Egyptian Voyage

TJ Michaels

ISBN: 0-9857874-2-2
ISBN-13:978-0-9857874-2-4

DEDICATION

This book is dedicated to the two coolest people on earth,
Tamara and Michael. For your understanding, inspiration
and lots and lots of midnight tea runs, I appreciate you.

AUTHOR NOTE

Dear Reader,

I wrote this book during the early stages of my career as a writer. When the rights reverted from the publisher back to me my first thought was to rewrite it. After some consideration I realized that I've grown as a writer and rewriting this book would basically result in a completely different style and story. So, here is Egyptian Voyage in its original form. Enjoy!

Love always,

~TJ

THE EMPRESS III

She is the celestial Isis. Nature, universal fecundity united with spiritual rectitude. She is fertility, creation, intelligence and activity. Whatever the gender, the Empress year brings you in touch with your need to nurture and be nurtured. She is Earth-Mother incarnate. The Empress is not just about love—she's about creativity planted in the realm of the imagination. She is fertile, ripe and blossoming, with ideas, plans, creations.

But know this, my friend—the upside-down Empress III tarot card has a completely different meaning. If the card is drawn by a woman, the upside-down Empress can represent that woman and indicate a partial success in regard to something important to her. But, if drawn by a man, it indicates a loss of love. Negative elements of the Empress are tendencies to be overbearing, vain, and using appearance to sway and manipulate.

And in our story, this Empress is not drawn by a woman. Nor is it drawn in the typical manner of right-side up. Looks like we've got a bad guy to put down...

PROLOGUE

Eden sat in the dark in his favorite overstuffed chair in the living room. The local news droned on while a small blue ticker scrolled across the bottom of the screen. He usually watched the screen with more than a little interest in the latest mayhem plaguing whatever port the ship happened to dock at. Tonight, the words of the news anchor, spoken in perfect Portuguese, rolled off him as he idly stroked the smooth bald head of the woman sitting quietly in his lap. She was twenty-six inches of porcelain perfection, clothed in the regalia of ancient Egypt and her station. Today, he'd clothed her in the white fine linen of the traditional shendyt kilt, leaving her caramel brown breasts bare.

He'd had her created with the face of the noble pharaoh, Hatshepsut. Perfectly formed lips and cheeks were free of rouge or coloring. Almond-shaped dark eyes were adorned with even darker liner that brought her face to life. Yes, she was definitely his favorite, his harem master, responsible for keeping the males in his harem in line. Not only was she beautiful and damned good at her job, her ability to interpret the tarot made her beyond valuable. Perhaps he'd keep her long enough to give her a name of his choosing.

Tilting his head, he contemplated the large tarot cards spread out on the coffee table. The surface of each was an exquisite work of art and displayed majestic Egyptian symbols of men and women who'd once ruled the ancient world. Their noble profiles brought a sense of kingship and kinship to him. The background of each was a mix of bold gold, turquoise and lapis blues laid over woven papyrus and set against a midnight deep black. Eying the beautiful tarot, the man stretched out a single finger and stroked the intricate borders of two that were separate from the rest of the deck.

Today, he'd drawn Strength and Justice.

"Yes, beloved, you are both."

He looked away from the cards and into the lovely face of the woman who'd spoken into his mind. He still hadn't figured out how she managed to do that. He could only hear her when she was near, but none of the others before her had ever been able to do even that much. She spoke again, her voice as clear as a summer sky in his head.

"The cards proclaim you to be Strength and Justice, to bring balance to this world."

Everything Eden did had the tarot at its center. He never made a move without consulting them. Today, he looked directly at the cards, saw what they were. But what did they mean? It seemed the interpretation of the cards was almost always different from what he intuitively thought it should be. But his Egyptian golden-skinned beauty always explained it all.

"Justice," she began in her smooth, seductive voice, *"is represented by a woman clad in white, a sword in one hand and a balance in the other. She sits on a throne with two lions at her feet. Strength is shown by a woman with a winged golden headdress, clothed in a white robe trimmed with turquoise jewels. A lion stands before her with the headdress of a pharaoh on his head. Strength holds the beast's mouth closed and he can go no further."*

Okay, so what?

"Strength, my beloved, is a card of success as long as you retain your instincts and exercise self-control. Justice indicates that all is going as it should. Even if you do not realize it, you're operating according to a divine plan. This plan is in harmony with you, my love, as well as correctness in your relationships."

Placing a gentle kiss on the top of his harem mistress's head, his mouth lifted in a wide satisfied smile. All of it sounded wonderful.

"So, who is my goal this time?" he queried, as the usual excitement kindled at the base of his gut. There was nothing like the anticipation of what was to come.

"There is a woman who has unbalanced the life of an important male. Her hair is a burnished hue and…"

When he'd memorized the description of the female, he rose, placed the harem mistress back on her shelf at the top of the beveled glass cabinet and left the ship. Now he could hunt with precision.

Later that night, as his prey screamed into a hand held firmly over her mouth, he did indeed feel the imbalance of the world shift and groan until it settled into its proper place. The specimen's sticky blood ran out of a fat hole in her back. It soaked through his shirt and streamed hot and thick over the ridges of his stomach, down to his navel. Yes, all was as it should be.

In spite of his ruined clothes, his chest puffed out with pride when the female took her final breath. Yes, once again he'd brought balance to the world and exacted justice on behalf of all those who depended on him as the rightful protector of the faith.

CHAPTER ONE

Chrysalyn Geyer yanked a large suitcase off the floor and let it bounce on the edge of the bed. Throwing open the top, she yanked out a pair of white capri pants, arranged them so they draped dead center in the middle of the hanger, then snapped them on the pole in the closet.

"What the hell am I supposed to do for three months, damn it?" she fumed, not bothering to send her thoughts psychically to her spirit guide.

Rest is a novel idea. I do believe it is the reason your employer sent you on this vacation.

"Adonei, do you always have to be so frickin' logical?" she growled between clenched teeth. Neatly folding her favorite cashmere sweater, she placed it on one of several wide shelves in the walk-in closet.

Of course. I am, after all, a male. Are we not the more logical of the species?

"Is this a trick question?" she chuckled, her tone incredulous. A balled-up fist made its way to her hip at the same time her bare foot tapped impatiently on the thick carpet. And how the hell had she wound up with a male for a spirit guide anyway? Perhaps the Great Spirit was testing her?

I believe it is time for a nap. Summon me if you have need, my dear. With a yawn and an exaggerated feline stretch, Adonei retreated to a small corner of her consciousness.

"Damned lion," she grumbled, already bored out of her mind.

No doubt this cruise ship was stellar. Everyone on board owned their oversized apartments. And according to the receptionist that checked her in yesterday afternoon, every single one of the units was built specifically for the owner, all of them larger than her whole house back in the States. And priced around a cool million dollars. Her company owned the sprawling condo she would occupy during her vacation. Way to go, Aegis.

Every outfit and its corresponding pair of shoes were arranged by color in the massive closet. Sigh. One more suitcase left, but it could wait until after a wash-up. Chrysalyn made her way to the stylish all-blue granite bathroom and flipped on the shower with a huff.

She had plenty of books but there was no way reading and doing the touristy thing at each port would keep her entertained for three blasted months. Thankfully, they were putting out to sea later on tonight, finally leaving the port in Lisbon, Portugal, behind. At least there would be a change of scenery. She'd also met a dashing older gentleman at the Japanese restaurant up on deck ten last night. Boy, was he a looker—a classic tall, dark and handsome man with a notably square jaw and the most exotic features she'd ever seen on a man.

His chin sported a perfectly manicured goatee over smooth-looking, tanned skin. And the cutest little dimple on his left cheek when he smiled. Salt-and-pepper hair, almost as dark and curly as her own, was stylishly cut. The man's name was Eden, an interesting name for a learned and well-traveled man. Wherever he was from, he was damned fine, in a sexy, Sean Connery, older gentleman kind of way.

Unfortunately, when he'd strolled over to her table and

asked to join her for dinner, a cold streak penetrated the very bones of her spine and chilled the nerves clear down to the backs of her knees. Not fear, but something else, something she couldn't put her finger on. The kicker was the fact that the emotions weren't hers, but Adonei's.

After ten minutes of enduring Adonei's roaring, growling and pacing in her head with no explanations, Chrysalyn pushed the apprehension away and pleaded with the lion to stand down and calm himself. Instead of listening to her, he'd charged to the forefront of her mind with a snarl so ferocious it caught her completely off guard. With fangs bared, the tawny hair on the back of his thick neck stood on end. And Chrys had bitten her lip and forced her butt to stay in the seat rather than jump to her feet in shock. What the hell was wrong with the big cat? He acted as if she was out on a case looking for bad guys, instead of dining in a classy shipboard restaurant, surrounded by highfalutin people and keeping company with a handsome, well-mannered man.

After practically inhaling her dinner and nodding through most of the conversation, Chrysalyn had smiled politely when Eden offered to see her to her apartment, relieved when he departed with a gentlemanly goodnight.

A full day later, she had yet to learn what Adonei found objectionable about Eden. Perhaps then she could see him again. In truth, she had no urge to fuck him whatsoever, but already looked forward to sharing more conversation. Maybe they could take in a movie or go for a stroll when they reached the next port? She was actually feeling rather encouraged about it all…

Until she'd returned from a brief foray into Lisbon, walked through her front door and locked it behind her. One look across the massive apartment reminded her she'd be floating in this private condo complex for another two months, twenty-eight days and four hours. Shit!

Tonight, determined to finish arranging things to her liking, she'd dined alone. The private chef service was awesome. Not only could she skip dressing up to eat, but a gorgeous Belgian chef had come to her room and prepared her dinner. Feeling rather catty, Chrys tried to trip him up and asked for something decidedly non-European. She'd ended up with the most delicious Cajun dishes piled in front of her with no idea where to begin the scrumptious fare. Her favorites, Shrimp Creole, crawfish bisque, hot water cornbread, fried oysters and okra were attacked with gusto. Perfectly seasoned so they weren't too spicy, she'd eaten until she was sure she'd have to summon Adonei onto this plane to drag her to her bedroom. Then the chef had sprung another one on her—fresh bananas foster flambéed to perfection before her eyes. Could she get any closer to heaven than soul food?

Now that she'd successfully waddled to the master bedroom to finish unpacking, she was so full it had taken her a full hour to get one huge bag unpacked. Now Chrysalyn stood underneath the massaging spray of the shower, conjuring up images of her first day back at work. She couldn't wait to return home to Denver and give her boss a piece of her mind. They'd already had the knockdown, drag-out fight of the century, which obviously hadn't done any good, considering Chrysalyn had still ended up on this damned boat headed for a much-too-long vacation on the high seas.

Who cared if she would visit ports in countries she'd never expected to see in her lifetime? What difference did it make that she hadn't had a vacation in five years? Who needed a vacation when you could spend every day of your life making a difference in the world by taking down bad guys?

Well, according to her boss, Geri, *she* needed one. And like it or not, she was getting one.

* * * * *

Dumping the pile of bloodied and soiled clothing into the laundry room hamper, Eden strolled gloriously naked into the luxurious bathroom. The blast of massaging showerheads eased his tense and aching muscles. The woman had put up quite a struggle—funny, his muscles were tight from working out yesterday morning, rather than the grisly business he'd been about only hours before. A perfect smile of perfect, straight white teeth split his lips. It had been the best hunt ever, though too short, too quick. And, like his smile, perfect. Guaranteed to loosen even the most stubborn bloodstains, he washed with the special soap he favored and watched the dried blood mix with steaming hot water and flow down the drain in a froth of pink-tinged bubbles. Eden lathered up again. A deep contentment stole over him as he inhaled. The fragrance was simply inspirational—a blend of vanilla and sandalwood. It was his female's favorite scent. No surprise, since she was the one who'd taught him how to make it.

"*Beloved?*"

"Yes, my dear?" he called over his shoulder, wishing she would leave him alone so he could make his dinner date on time. Truthfully, he couldn't really call it a date, since the woman he planned to meet had no idea he would be joining her. The hunt had taken all damned day. He was in a hurry and now was no time to chatter.

Dressed in classic black dress slacks, tailored black dinner jacket, a crisp white silk shirt and black silk tie, he strode out into the living room. Not bothering to sit down to draw his hand, Eden's long strong fingers stretched toward the deck of gold and black Egyptian tarot cards stacked neatly in the middle of the coffee table. The card on top was snatched up and tossed to the center of the table. The III card—The Empress. Quirking his head to the side, Eden spoke to his faithful companion.

"Why is she upside down? I've never drawn The Empress card upside down before." Actually, he'd never drawn the Empress in any case. A strange chill chased down his spine as he took in the regal form and features of the dark golden goddess pictured on the card.

"*I am sure it is nothing, beloved. Come, kiss me before you go about tonight's business."*

Eden walked over to the display case and gently lifted his most prized possession down from her glass perch.

"Hurry, beloved." The sweet caress of her voice eased over his soul like the soothing warmth of a summer sun shower sweeping across the fertile Nile plains. Strange how that same voice sometimes bordered on sheer annoyance. *"Kiss me, so you may go and return to me again."*

Running his fingers over the smooth cool skin of her arms, he looked deeply into the dark, almond-shaped eyes. He loved the charcoal outline on her lids and brows, and the slim angular classic Egyptian features. Eden kissed the pharaoh gently on the top of her head, his emotions catapulting between excitement and sadness. He tucked his nose beneath her chin, careful not to disturb the pharaoh's headdress, an exquisite lapis and gold rearing cobra settled low over her brow.

He knew she cared for him, but while he'd followed all of her advice, he was no fool and was well aware of her true intentions. Every female she'd directed him to dispense justice upon seemed the perfect lover for one of the males in his harem. She wanted to be the only one to rule their little clan and would do whatever it took to see that it stayed that way. After all, she had the spirit of a man, thus was she pharaoh. Not a queen, but a king.

Thoughts turned to the woman he'd spotted boarding the ship in Lisbon yesterday afternoon. Now *she* was the perfect Egyptian queen. A couple of evenings past, he'd managed to *accidentally* run into her at one of the ship's restaurants. Tonight, he hoped to bump into her again.

While the beauty had been dressed inappropriately for his tastes, he couldn't help but admire her form—and such an itty-bitty thing, perhaps five foot three at the most. Shapely legs teased him from the hem of her sleeveless little black dress down to her cute little sandal-clad toes. Broad shoulders and toned arms supported full, inviting breasts that tapered down to a trim waist. When she'd excused herself to run to the ladies' room, he'd watched every step. Her hips flared lusciously and her ass was indescribably tempting. Round, wide and firm would do for starters. His fingers itched just thinking about touching all that caramel skin. Delicious.

When she'd turned and laid a stunning smile on him, his breathing had deepened on the spot as all the blood in his torso streaked down to his groin. Beauty was too tame a word—the woman was exquisitely breathtaking. Thick black hair was a riot of twists and curls all over her head. He didn't typically like short hair on a woman, but this woman's shiny, healthy-looking waves looked just perfect for running his fingers through. Her eyes were a mix of light brown and gold, contrasting against her dark skin. In the end, he couldn't decide what color they were, only that they were just as lovely as the rest of her.

And the aura emanating from her pulsed with life. Chrysalyn was her name. And she was perfect for bearing strong sons.

Beloved?

The voice bounced him out of his reverie. He looked down at the one who called him beloved. The rare creation cradled in his hands was impeccable and unique. Her long braids and golden winged breastplate were indicative of her heritage—a goddess, a daughter of pharaohs. But even her loveliness paled when compared to Chrysalyn, whose very name referred to new life. No, he simply could not allow his harem mistress to ruin his plans to mate another. And Chrysalyn would be that woman.

With that firmly in his mind, he stood and cast a final glance at the tarot card on the table as he made his way across the room. He placed the harem mistress back into the glass display case with his other unique creations.

Her voice trickled over him once more.

"*Enjoy your dinner. Until tonight, beloved.*"

On the way out, he looked back at the beautiful work of porcelain perfection and blew her a kiss. Headed for the on-board Japanese restaurant, his step quickened as his thoughts filled with the possibilities between him and the female he was hopefully on his way to meet.

CHAPTER TWO

Jerked out of a sound sleep, Chrysalyn's eyes flew open as her heart beat wildly in her chest. Lying perfectly still, surrounded by a pile of oversized pillows and warm blankets, she looked around the empty bedroom. There was no sound except the muted splash of the ocean's waves against the hull as the huge ship cut through the water.

She sighed with a bit of frustration mixed with relief. At least they were on the way somewhere and not still sitting in port, as they had the last couple of days since she'd boarded.

"*Adonei? Adonei, come to me,*" she silently whispered. Seconds ticked by. No answer. No Adonei.

Where the hell was that damned lion? In all the long years he'd watched over and guided her, he'd never failed to come when summoned.

Well, spirit guide or not, her innate senses told her something was wrong. Reaching out along the psychic bond they shared, she tried again, calling quietly, but firmly, in her mind.

Annoyed, Chrys gave up on the psychic thing and opened her mouth. "Adonei, get here already," she snapped on an impatient whisper.

Finally, the still air shimmered and shifted next to the bed as Adonei appeared shaking his wild mane on a loud, wide-mouthed yawn. Chrysalyn was glad no one else could hear the racket. Lord, he had a big mouth, all sharp teeth and power. Glad he was on her side, she smiled with genuine affection at her companion as the moonlight streamed through the floor-to-ceiling glass deck doors, reflecting off his two-and-a-half-inch canines. Adonei—African lion and *male* to the bone. No wonder this creature was the king of beasts.

Chrysalyn, what is it now? Surely you did not summon me to this plane to complain about your three-month rest again?

Okay, so he was a cynical king of beasts.

'Adonei, I heard something. Well, not actually heard, but definitely felt. Someone's in here.'

He didn't say a word. No change of expression, no smart-assed remark, nothing. Now she definitely knew something was going on. Fine, she'd just have to see for herself.

'Adonei, lend me your sight.'

Take what I offer, he yawned.

Geesh, was he ever rattled by anything? Guess not.

Keeping her eyes open and focused on her bedroom door, Chrysalyn embraced Adonei's gifts as they flowed warm and comforting underneath her skin before sinking into her blood. The strength and power of the lion burst forth and filled her. Human eyes took on superhuman clarity as the dim shadows of the night receded and all became perfectly clear. Whispering an unladylike, but appropriate, blue streak of curses, she grumbled under her breath and climbed out of bed. Whoever had disturbed her sleep would royally pay for it. On bare feet, she eased her way across the room to the sliding glass door that opened onto the private deck.

The metal handle was cool against her fingers as she slid the door open. Thankfully, it was well-oiled and moved silently along its rails. Poking her head through the small opening, she eyed the entire length of the moonlit deck before stepping out into the balmy night. All was quiet. The pitch-black sky overhead was blanketed with a sea of stars so vast it rivaled the twinkling of the moon off the surface of the water stretching out before the ship. If she hadn't been scooting across the deck in the middle of an emergency, she would have sank down into the nearest cushioned deck chair and slipped back into her dreams under those stars.

But nooo! Instead of enjoying the relaxing atmosphere, the lull of the waves, the pearlescent glow of the moon, she had to kick someone's ass tonight for breaking into her apartment.

Kneeling down, she peeked through the far deck door into the dim living room.

"Oh, you just wait," she ground out between clenched teeth, her spiking temper directed at the dark shadow easing into the guest bedroom. Her head cocked sideways in surprise when the shadow reappeared and moved toward her closed bedroom door.

She eased the glass door open a crack, thankful for the lack of sea breeze. The last thing she needed was for the drapes to billow and warn the bastard of his impending ass-kicking.

The second his head disappeared through the opening of her bedroom door, the living room pane slid all the way open and Chrysalyn flew toward the encroacher on silent feet.

The closer she got to the shadow, the more it stretched toward the high ceilings. It was a man, and whoever he was, he was tall and well-built. Fine, she'd just have to take him down hard and fast. Damn it, now she wished she'd asked Adonei for his strength instead of just his exceptional sight. But she didn't have time for that now.

With a well-aimed kick at the common peroneal nerve running along the intruder's right leg, she struck out with all her strength. In a fraction of a second, the leg went numb and buckled, unable to support the man's weight. As he went down, a solid uppercut connected with his jaw, followed by a lightning-fast left to the mouth. But before she could finish him, Chrysalyn found herself wrapped in a tangle of arms and legs, and heading swiftly toward a meeting with the hardwood floor. The intruder rolled with her until the legs of the coffee table blocked their progress, with him on top. Damn.

She looked up into a handsome face a mere three inches from her own. Holy shit! Even in the dark, there was no mistaking the perpetrator's identity. After three years apart, there still wasn't another male who looked like this. Felt like this. Smelled like this.

"Rahn!" she gasped, from both shock and exertion. "What the hell are you doing here?"

"At the moment, I'm bleeding. How are you, Chrysalyn?"

Oooh, and his voice was still dead sexy. Double damn!

* * * * *

"Rahn? What the hell are you doing here?"

"Well, now that you've asked so sweetly," he huffed sarcastically, a bit winded by their tussle. At least his leg was beginning to get the feeling back. Ow! His ribs hurt too. She'd kicked the shit out of him. He took as deep a breath as he was able, and said, "I have a case to close in Rome. Since the ship was headed there anyway, Geri thought I might enjoy a little holiday first. It's been awhile since the last one."

"Vacation? Here? With me?" The woman was practically screeching. If he didn't know better, he'd swear she was nervous about him sharing the huge apartment. He'd have to ask his spirit guide about it later. Man, she felt good underneath him. Time to move before he gave away just *how* good she felt. Rolling away, he immediately missed the warmth of her body.

"This is the company's apartment. With three

bedrooms and a couple thousand square feet, it's more than big enough. Our boss figured you wouldn't mind."

On his feet now, Rahn headed for the nearest couch. A glance over his shoulder made his body shudder. The woman was still spread-eagled on her back. Her itty-bitty nightshirt didn't cover much, bunched up just below her sex as it was. He cocked his head and spoke silently to his spirit guide.

'Mahpiya, lend me your senses.'

Immediately, the lioness's gifts flooded into him. Ooh, big mistake. He tightened his thigh muscles, trying to keep from coming on the spot when his eyesight sharpened and Mahpiya's sharp sense of smell flooded through his body until it became his own. His eyes took in the sleek, smooth length of Chrysalyn's lovely legs. His nose told him she lay sprawled on the floor, minus any kind of panties. The scent of her pussy wafted through the air and practically sucked all the common sense right out of his head. Sweet, deliciously sensual, her scent was reminiscent of honeysuckle and dark red wine.

"Shit," he grumbled, realizing the couch wasn't nearly far enough away from her. He eased toward a chair clear across the huge room. He flopped down into the overstuffed cushions, snatched a pillow from behind his head and smashed it down over a suddenly painful erection. Where the hell had the hard-on from hell come from?

Did you not ask for my aid, my charge?

'Oh shut it, Mahpiya,' he quipped at his psychic companion. Damned cat had no mercy.

Do not be angry with me, youngling. I gave you just what you asked for. 'Tis no fault of mine you received more than you bargained for.

Then she laughed! How the hell did a lioness laugh anyway? Damn it, she was supposed to be his spirit guide, not his tormenter.

You torment yourself, young one.

Rahn was thankful when she retreated into a small corner of his mind to nap. But not before she sent a genuinely amused and toothy grin through their psychic bond. Damned cat.

Chrys' words broke through his thoughts. "So, why are you going to Rome?"

His eyes were drawn toward the lovely body projecting the silky voice across the room. Lifting his head, he glanced her way. Shit, she was still on the floor, only now her arms were crossed behind her head as she looked toward the clear glass doors that led out to the deck.

"Rahn? Did you hear me?"

Hell no, he hadn't heard her. He was too busy trying to drown out the blood rushing through his ears as it streaked toward his dick.

"What did you say? My head hurts from the pounding you did on it. Hard to focus," he lied—about the focus part, not about the pounding. He watched her roll up from the floor and stomp her way to the chair across from him. She flopped down in it, completely nonplussed, comfortable in her practically bare skin and obviously unaware how delicious she looked.

"I asked what you're going to be doing in Rome, Rahn," she said.

Okay, time to get his head together to make this lie sound convincing. As much as he hated to tell her half-truths, if the woman ever found out the nature of the case he was on his way to solve, he'd never be able to keep her nose out of it.

"There have been a string of murders there. They seem to be centered around a certain area. The international police have asked us to look into it for them. Less complicated if we investigate the matter, since our organization flies well below the radar." The last few words were said with a grunt as he shifted on the chair and tried to rearrange his cock in his pants.

"So," he gasped as his fingers wrapped around his

raging hard-on, pushing it to the left. "How's that gorgeous cousin of yours?"

"Delaine? She's fine. Getting married soon."

Now that snapped him and his cock to attention. Delaine Jeris was getting remarried? Whoever had landed that beauty was a lucky man. Rahn was glad she'd finally let go of that idiot she'd been married to for so long and moved on. Everyone in their agency had been tempted to help the asshole have a little accident after word got around about what he'd done to Delaine. If their boss, Geri, hadn't expressly forbade any late-night ass-kickings for the man, he would have been nothing but a pile of sore bones for ages to come.

"She met someone soon after she moved out to Charlotte," Chrysalyn said, her voice somewhat wispy, as if she longed for something. But she was getting married herself. So why did she sound so…forlorn?

"Speaking of married," Rahn said quietly, watching her closely. "You've been engaged for a while now. When is your big date?"

As quickly as she'd sat down, she was back on her feet. Back stiff with what could only be a major case of ticked off, she stomped across the floor, into her bedroom and slammed a solid wood door on him without a word.

"Well, hell, that didn't go as planned," he grumbled to himself.

Mahpiya's powerful presence surged to the forefront of his mind until he could see the outline of her majestic feline form just behind his eyes.

Do not fret, my charge. It is not your fault. She is lonely.

"Lonely?" What the hell kind of sense did that make? The woman was getting married. How could she be lonely?

She is lonely because she is not getting married. She is alone and in need of comfort.

His eyebrows rose so fast, surely they would fly off his face and hit the ceiling. With narrowed eyes and more than a bit of serious curiosity, he practically growled at his psychic companion.

"How do you know she's not getting married, Mahpiya?"

Rahn sent utter shock resonating down the bond he shared with Mahpiya. He rolled his eyes in frustration as the image of the majestic lioness, lying in a comfortable heap licking her huge paws, faded from behind his eyes without answering his question.

* * * * *

The ship was underway on the three-day sail from Lisbon to the Balearic Islands in the south of Spain. It meant hunting on board until they made port. He didn't particularly care for it. There weren't enough dim or dark nooks to hide, which meant there just weren't as many opportunities to genuinely enjoy stalking his prey.

His breathing quickened at the remembered thought of how the last woman had looked over her shoulder, her body stiff with fear when she'd realized that someone followed her. He'd stalked her for the entire time they'd been in port in Lisbon, all ten days. Each evening she'd walked from the middle of town to a small flat. Each night, her apprehension had grown more and more acute until he'd thought he might be able to reach out and eat a piece of it.

His cock swelled as his mind conjured the wide-eyed dread etched across her lovely features when he'd finally shown himself. He'd known the exact second she realized her life approached its end. Her last gasp, the last thump of her heart had brought with it such a heady rush of adrenaline, accompanied by a high so consuming he felt it down to his shoelaces. And he craved it again, would have it again.

Eden moved quietly through his bedroom to the closet where he gently stroked the black silk he so loved to wear. It never showed the blood and cleaned up nicely.

At sea, there were no pretty little females to follow

through the darkness of the night or stalk from dark alleys. No overconfident, swaggering young men to approach in the gathering dark. No matter. There were plenty of people who considered themselves high class, and too good to mate with the men in his harem. It would be easy to keep his skills sharpened on them. He would simply practice on a hand-picked pawn aboard ship. After all, it was the sole reason they were on board, for his pleasure.

"At it again, I hear," he mumbled to himself with a shake of his head and gently closed the bedroom door at the first screech of his harem mistress's voice. She was no doubt on the case of one of the men again, scolding in a tone she never, ever used with him. Then again, she may be scolding them all.

"You will say nothing to our master," her hard voice practically cut the air around her. "I am responsible for all of you and this is not outside the realm of my authority. I will deal with it," said the lovely Egyptian female who called him "Beloved". She was indeed responsible for the harem. In spite of her tendency to dominate those she was supposed to care for, she'd said nothing that caused him concern. Eden ignored the conversation. Whatever the issue, let her deal with it.

Dressed in severe black, the only break in the darkness around his body was a crisp, blinding white silk handkerchief expertly tucked into the top pocket of his dinner jacket. Clasping an onyx cufflink onto the sleeve of his black shirt, Eden made his way through the living room and over to his most prized possessions to make sure all was well before he stepped out for the evening.

They were sullen, but otherwise unharmed. Eden picked them up one by one and allowed them to touch his mind, speak to him about their troubles. First was the porcelain, bronze-skinned male he called Shaman. A prized Native American warrior, with a body so perfectly sculpted even he would have been tempted if the man were flesh and blood. He was beautiful, standing at almost twenty-four-inches tall, with perfect porcelain skin and jet black hair down to his solid waist. And as usual, the first thoughts he shared with his master were of how much he resented having to bow to the whims of a temperamental female harem mistress, no matter how exquisite.

After a few assuring words, Eden put Shaman back on the shelf and reached for the next work of perfection.

Celon was a blond-haired Viking if there ever was one. A little shorter than Shaman, he stood at twenty-three inches of porcelain perfection. Dressed in classic Norwegian garb reminiscent of the early ninth century, he sported a wide muscular chest, a narrow waist and thick legs. His expression was one of seduction. His creator must have been a female. Even one painted eyebrow was raised in invitation and one side of his perfect mouth tilted up into a sly smile. He was a predator, plain and simple. Yes, he was Eden's favorite.

After listening to Celon's short, clipped complaint about the pharaoh harem mistress, Eden smiled at the man as a final thought slipped into his mind. Celon wanted nothing more than to fuck the harem mistress silly until she gladly got on her knees and begged him to take her. Poetic justice, since that was her favorite position for all ten males in the harem—on their knees before her.

But Eden could not regret her behavior. He needed someone ruthless to keep his stable in line. And what was more ruthless than a female?

Last, he picked up Daven. The dark-skinned male reminded him of the Egyptian kings. More than once, he thought he'd spotted the figure of this doll on one of the tarot cards he studied. Egypt was, after all, in Africa. It would be no surprise to find a man like this exquisite creation as a former ruler of that amazing place. Skin as darkly smooth as his favorite coffee, Daven was a master of temptation, as were all of the men in his collection. Dark brown eyes set under even darker brows practically beckoned females to his bed. If he were standing before him in the flesh Eden might have even considered asking him for advice on securing the female, Chrysalyn.

Tonight Daven was clearly not in the mood to play. And, for once, he didn't want to fuck the harem mistress. He wanted to beat her senseless. Why? The bitch had again selected a female for elimination that would have made a perfect mate for one in the harem.

His Japanese doll, Saraka, was enraged and distraught. The last woman the harem mistress had instructed Eden to hunt and ultimately destroy should have been Saraka's mate.

Oh well, nothing to be done about it now. Eden said goodnight to all of his men and lifted the harem mistress from her perch. With her in his arms, he made a beeline for the couch in the massive living room and reached out to the stack of tarot.

What the hell? The Empress upside down again. Pinning his harem mistress with a hard stare, he pushed the words out of his mouth.

"What does this card mean when it's not upside down?" he asked with an even, calm tone, though apprehension slipped down the backs of his legs.

It represents the woman who is important to you. As a male, it may be a woman you know or will meet who may become your friend, lover or mate. It may also mean that you are entering a time of overflow, abundance and prosperity.Opportunities may very well come upon you from out of nowhere, she replied quietly, carefully.

"Yes, but if all this comes about when the Empress is right side up, then the upside-down card must mean I am headed for trouble," Eden pressed roughly, unfamiliar with the apprehension twitching around in his gut. And he didn't like it one bit. He knew only one thing—his Egyptian flower had better tell him what he wanted to hear.

If this card pertained to you, then perhaps what you say is true. However, I do not believe you are selecting this card for yourself, but for a person you have yet to come across. Perhaps this card tells us the future of your next task? she said in a soothing timbre.

"You'd better fucking be right," he said calmly, kissing her lightly on each brow. With less than two hours before the ship left port, tonight he had to be precise in order to handle his business and get back on board in time.

Easing open her resting place, Eden set her gently on the top shelf of the glass cabinet and asked, "So, who shall it be tonight?" He stroked the top of her glossy head, loving the silky slide of her ethnic braids through his fingers. He paused mid-stroke and pinned her with a level stare. "And no more targeting the females who are meant for the men."

Her angry sigh echoed in his head, but he knew she would not gainsay him. At least not out loud.

CHAPTER THREE

"Nope, definitely not a morning person," Rahn moaned to himself. Damn, even floating on water with the sun beaming into his room, warm and bright, he still wanted nothing more than to stuff the pillow over his head and tell the day to go to hell.

Well, no hope for it. He had a case to solve and a woman to protect. And that woman, who had always risen with the chickens, was no doubt up and about. Too bad he couldn't protect her in bed. Hmmm, then again, she was single again. Just maybe…

Kicking the covers off with a loud huff, Rahn pushed to his feet and stood there a moment. The view through the huge beveled glass window no more than three feet from his bed was incredible. He could see past the private deck and out to sea, where the sun shone down from a clear sky. The light reflected off the dark blue water, causing it to sparkle like the finest London blue topaz gems. And there was nothing else but ocean and more ocean. God, he hated deep water. Anything deeper than a bathtub was out of his comfort zone. If the ship went down on its way through the Mediterranean straits, it would be all he could do to stay afloat long enough to be rescued. And it was going to take three whole days to get to Ibiza? Damn.

Well, at least the ship was large enough that he wouldn't be constantly bent over the railing feeding the fish every time he had a bite to eat. With a snort, he dragged himself to his private bath.

Already bored, his mind sought for something to think on besides the case that brought him here. But until he checked in with his boss, Geri, for an intel update there was no need to dwell on it.

His thoughts drifted to Chrysalyn and the bomb Mahpiya had dropped on him last night. Chrysalyn was lonely? He still didn't understand it.

"Mah, come to me," he whispered around his toothbrush. At least his eyes were open and he was beginning to recall how to focus. Damn, he was tired. Mahpiya eased to the forefront of his mind, the slabs of dense muscle under her tawny coat flexing as she moved. He closed his eyes a second and grinned when the great cat flopped down on her stomach, raised her amber eyes and waited for him to speak.

Glad no one was around, so that he could speak out loud, Rahn jumped right in and said, "I wonder what the hell happened to Chrysalyn, Mah. I mean, the last time I saw her, she was engaged to that asshole, Kevin or Calvin or something like that. What the bloody hell went down? It's times like this I wish you could pop over to wherever she is and read her mind."

Shaking his head in wonder, he was still unable to believe the one woman he knew he couldn't live without was somewhere around this sprawling apartment. And she was available. Heading for the shower, he stopped short at Mahpiya's next words.

There is no need for mind reading. Chrysalyn Geyer is your mate.

Whoa! Back up. Rahn spun around so fast the clear glass door to the huge stall he'd just opened smacked him soundly on the knuckles. Rubbing the now-tender skin, he reached into his mind, demanding an explanation.

"Mah, how the hell can you know that?" When she didn't immediately reply, he summoned the feline onto this plane so he could look her in the eyes. "Mahpiya, come to me. Right now."

The sleek African lioness disappeared from behind his eyes and shimmered into her corporeal form right in front of him. Damn, she was huge—four feet tall and almost four-hundred-eighty pounds of raw power. At the top of the food chain, her earthly cousins were the perfect hunters. And Mahpiya was no less formidable. With the ability to speak mind-to-mind with those in her care, Rahn tended to forget how majestically imposing Mahpiya was. He immediately lowered his head and asked her forgiveness for his impertinence. After all, she served him at her pleasure. He was blessed to have such a wise companion.

Stepping into the shower, he dunked his head under the lukewarm flow and exhaled sharply. The scent of his favorite sandalwood soap filled the oversized stall.

"Okay, Mah, what do you mean, Chrysalyn is my mate?" Could it be? Chrysalyn, the woman perfect for him? He should have been shocked, so why wasn't he? Because Chrysalyn had been everything he'd ever dreamed of in a woman, a real class act. All he'd had to do was pursue her. But noooo, he'd been an idiot and allowed himself to be, uh, distracted by woman who'd chased after him instead. He'd learned later that same woman not only pursued him, but any other cock she could get her hands on. Hell, she had even slept with his best friend. Claimed it was all part of the job as an undercover. Yeah, right.

Obviously, their relationship hadn't lasted, but by the time he'd pulled his head out of his ass, Chrysalyn had moved on to someone who treated her like she deserved. The two had been engaged to be married and the woman seemed happy enough. So what happened?

He was snapped out of his musings by Mahpiya's sharp words and sultry voice.

Get dressed, hoksila. *You must be about your business. Your mate awaits you.*

With that, Mahpiya herded him out of the shower and back into his room with an urgency that had him moving double time. Was something wrong? Was Chrysalyn in danger? And where the hell was the woman, anyway? And hadn't Mah mentioned a spirit guide before?

If you stop thinking, you can move faster, Mahpiya growled before swatting him across the backside with a large paw.

"Ouch! Damn it, that hurt," Rahn yelped, hoping the impending welts didn't cause him too much discomfort later. A faint sound caught his attention as he fished around for underwear and a pair of sport socks in his dresser drawer. Lifting his eyes toward the quiet splash, Rahn spied an unlikely vision through the glass doors leading out to the deck.

Holy shit! Chrysalyn basked under the early morning sunshine, her body partially hidden by the swirling rush of hot water in the oversized hot tub. Arms spread out to her sides, the swell of her breasts was just visible above the waterline. Her delicious, cinnamon skin gleamed enticingly, wet from the steam and droplets peppering her beautiful body. The leopard-print swimsuit plastered to her curves sent a rush of heat straight to his cock. Her hair was loose and little curls framed her strong jawline as she laid her head back, eyes closed and...puffed? On a cigar?

His cock screamed as he stood there, mute and unable to get a single muscle in his body to move. She was so damned sexy. And here he stood with another chance to have her and he couldn't draw his eyes away from the window.

Another swat across his buttocks took care of that.

"Okay, already! I'm going, Mah."

Excellent, she purred as her corporeal form shimmered away.

Not like he needed any further encouragement. One peek at the exquisite woman lounging in the tub had his dick stiffer and hotter than a fireplace poker left sitting on top of a burning log.

The next moment found Rahn moving toward the doors with sheer determination in his stride. He headed across the deck and straight toward the hot tub and the succulent woman awaiting him.

* * * * *

The second the hair started dancing on the back of her neck, Chrysalyn's brows drew together in a fierce frown. Forcing the muscles of her face to relax until she was the epitome of absolute calm, she called to her spirit guide.

Reaching out with her mind, she asked, 'Adonei, who's approaching?'

Do not worry, my charge. There is no danger.

'I don't give a shit if there's danger. I don't like people sneaking up on me.'

And who the hell wanted to admit the man was making plenty of noise. The loud snap of the glass doors to his room and the soft flap of his bare feet on the wood deck told her who approached. His fresh masculine scent stole over her, carried on the easy ocean breeze. Oh great! Now her stomach was doing the butterfly samba. What the hell was there to be so giddy about? It was only Rahn, right? It was only the man she should have married three years ago. The man whose smooth tenor English accent sent little strokes of heat up the back of her knees. Whose sexy smile and killer physique made her want to do all sorts of nasty things to him.

The bastard who fell for a horse-humping bitch who wanted nothing more than to prove she could steal him. And he'd fallen for it, the idiot.

Ease yourself, Chrysalyn. You are screaming in my ear, Adonei scolded with a deep growl. His annoyed expression was crystal clear in her head, along with the bored roll of his eyes. How an African lion managed to roll his eyes, she would never know. And she was *not* screaming, damn it!

"Chrysalyn?"

Sitting up, she opened her eyes and watched Rahn approach. Tangy ocean mist drifted up from the wake as the huge ship cut gently through the waves. It tickled her nose. She liked the way it smelled. The sun had risen only an hour before, but the deck was already nicely warmed and comfortable. Add the barely perceptible rocking of the sea and her day was perfect. But the vivid blues painted across the sky, the smell of the sea, the opulence of her private dwelling, all of it paled in comparison to the gloriously naked man coming her way. His stride was long, but easy, kind of reminding her of Adonei when he was hunting some imaginary prey.

The sweet chocolate and coffee smoke of her Kahlua cigar drifted like silken threads of aromatic decadence. The scent of the indulgence she enjoyed every now and again made her think of how long and thick the hand-rolled treat was, which in turn carried her wayward thoughts to other similarly shaped objects that would fit nicely perched between her lips. Aw, hell.

Reaching up, she plucked the fat Kahlua cigar from her lips and set it in the sleek ashtray just off to her left. Sounding as bored as Adonei's eye-rolling looked, her voice lacked any kind of warmth as she answered his call.

"Yeah, what, Rahn?"

There is no need to be rude, Chrysalyn. Adonei again. Didn't the cat have somewhere to go?

'Says who? I was perfectly fine out here all by myself. What the hell does he want anyway?' she grumbled back at her spirit guide, who was becoming more and more a pain in the backside lately with all his male logic.

He is not a danger to you, woman. However, that black-clothed fellow does concern me.

'Who? What black-clothed fellow?' she wondered.

The one who insinuated himself into your company when you were dining alone. That one is dangerous, I am sure of it.

'Eden, hmm? Seems harmless enough. But you've never steered me wrong. I would be a fool to totally ignore your warning. I'll be careful.'

Thank you. Now, in the meantime, you have company.

Hell, she'd almost forgotten about Rahn.

Geez, what a blatant lie. But that was her story and she was sticking to it. By the time her conversation with Adonei was done, Rahn was climbing into the hot tub with a determination in his eyes she was sure she'd never seen unless he was after a bad guy.

He was very close now. So close that if the water hadn't already been one-hundred-two degrees, she was sure the heat emanating from his body would have taken care of any tepidness. She sat up and looked down.

Oh dear lord. The man was gloriously naked, with a cock so long, broad and hard that the game of baseball came to mind. Hell, he was at least a foot away from her, but the thick-veined tool jutting her way put him a whole lot closer.

One more step and his erection thudded against her stomach, just underneath her breasts and partially hidden by the frothing water. Her heart rate kicked up into overdrive and breathing was a whole lot higher on the scale of important things to do. Okay, time to go. So, why weren't her legs carrying her the hell out of the damned hot tub?

"Chrysalyn?" he asked, seeking her permission to touch with a whisper-soft plea against the side of her face. With her butt rooted to the spot, she watched one of his large, strong hands move toward her face to remove her sunglasses as the other tipped her chin up just before his lips brushed sensuously against hers.

"Chrys, baby, I've missed you so much." His breath was a barrage of peppermint flowing over her cheek, followed by Eskimo kisses. When was the last time she'd rubbed noses with a man, or anyone for that matter?

His perfectly chiseled body scant inches from hers sent

the blood dancing in her veins as the heat in her own skin threatened to out heat the bubbling tub. God, why had he always been able to get to her like this? Especially when she should totally hate the bastard—the dark-haired, tawny-eyed, gorgeous and seemingly sincere bastard. The knowledge that he could move her like no one else pissed her off.

Or perhaps you are more angry with yourself? Adonei queried as he faded to a little corner of her mind.

Nope! She was not angry with herself. Even if she had made every dumb decision possible during that rocky period while on the rebound from Rahn. Even if he would have crawled back, she'd simply been too proud to forgive him, determined to stay with the fiancé from hell just to prove a point.

Oooh, but now he nibbled that little spot he knew she liked while whispering her name between little bites.

"God, Chrysalyn, you taste so good," he murmured against her slightly parted lips before covering her mouth with his. Any gentle intent dissolved into pure lust as he entangled his tongue with hers. She felt herself slip under his spell, felt the petals of her sex tingle and burn, and it had nothing to do with the heat of the hot tub.

Then she was suddenly empty. Rahn was there, but in her mind, she was utterly, totally alone.

Usually an expert at schooling her features, her emotions slipped out of her grasp and ran away from her. The panic that reared up to press against the middle of her chest was etched clearly across her face. Adonei! He was gone. They'd never been apart since the day she'd met him as a child. Why? Why now?

I am here, Chrysalyn, bu tI would not disrespect you or your mate by intruding upon your mating.

'What? Adonei, don't you dare leave me!' she wailed in her head.

Your mate will take good care of you. Do not worry. I will be near.

'My mate? What's with this mate stuff? Adonei? Come back!'

"Hey, sweetheart, what's wrong?" Rahn asked, letting her push away just a bit. The concern in his voice, accompanied by a little shake, broke through the wall of fear quickly erecting itself around her heart and snatched her back to the present.

"Are you all right?"

Her gut clenched painfully. All right? Hell no, she wasn't all right, but it would be a seven-below-zero day in hell before she admitted it. He couldn't possibly understand the emptiness in her head, the little void in her heart that was always filled with Adonei's presence. Just the thought of being alone inside her own mind was downright terrifying.

Rahn crooned into her ear, holding her tenderly, gently massaging the muscles of her back. "You look afraid. You know I won't hurt you, love."

Still shaken from Adonei's absence, she snapped, "I'm not afraid of you, Rahn." And moved to jump out of the tub.

Rahn's hand wrapped firmly around her biceps just as her toe hit the edge of the Jacuzzi. She froze.

"I'm sorry, Chrys. I didn't mean to upset you," he said quickly, his smooth voice full of concern. The pained expression in his deep amber eyes moved something buried inside her she'd thought long dead—the ability to receive comfort from a man. That comfort eased through her heart, mind and body, worked its way to her head and calmed her fears.

She went willingly into his arms, allowing herself to be cocooned against the solid wall of his chest. He picked her up and the natural masculine scent of his skin enveloped her as he eased her into his lap to straddle his hips.

Mmm, and his lips, soft and slightly damp from the steam rising from the water, tasted of fresh air, mint and warm aroused man. Then again, perhaps the meaty, throbbing erection bobbing up and down between them indicated the aroused part.

"Oh, baby, I've missed this. Missed just being close to you." The edginess in his voice made her thighs, draped over his, quiver like Japanese mochi pudding. The skin where their bodies touched melted clean away when he moved in for another kiss, this one hot and unapologetic. His need conveyed through the movement of his lips and tongue, the motion smooth, but hard, full of desire and heat. It made her want, made her need. Chrysalyn moaned wantonly as he practically inhaled her.

"Damn, woman, I want you more than I want to breathe," he whispered against the damp curls plastered against the side of her face.

"Really?" she gasped when he moved away from devouring her mouth to nip the sensitive spot just underneath her jawline. "You want me? Even more than…?"

"Yes, baby, I want you more than I ever wanted her."

How had he known what she was going to say? Then again, he'd always known what she was feeling, thinking. It was as if they'd simply picked up where they left off three years ago. Last night, she'd fled from him, hadn't wanted to explain her breakup with her ex-fiancé. And she certainly hadn't wanted to acknowledge how the old spark between them emerged to hum just below her skin the moment she'd come up on him sneaking around her apartment.

Now that spark flared like a newly lit stack of charcoal doused with lighter fluid. The strong feelings she'd stuffed under mounds of work and duties crashed to the surface as if they'd never been buried.

His hands slid across her steam-slick skin, pausing to knead a muscle here and there, reminding her of the most decadent massage she'd ever had in her life. One he'd given her long ago. One she'd never forgotten and never thought to experience again. And there was nothing she could think of to compare it to. Hell, she could barely think at all.

"Baby, please. Let me taste you?" he asked in a way that wasn't really a request. And boy, did she ever want to feel his mouth on her. Her teeth snapped together with an audible *click* at the feel of his tongue, wet and hot, sliding up her neck to lick away the moisture along the way.

"Chrys?" he asked again. "Let me?"

Yes, oh, yes. She wanted to give him permission, but when the slightly roughened pads of his fingers eased underneath the wet fabric of the slinky little two-piece and skimmed along her ass, she couldn't get a single word out. All she could do was nod her head and hope he was paying attention. Could he taste her? Hell yes!

With Mahpiya's subtle retreat to the outermost reaches of his mind, Rahn's head was strangely empty, yet at the same time, full of Chrysalyn—the way her short silky curls reflected the morning sun, the contrast of her milk chocolate skin against his tanned fairer tones. And her height, the little firebrand was so much shorter than him. Even when he lifted her out of the water, set her on the edge of the hot tub and kneeled on the seat in front of her, they were still of a height. Her breasts were just enough decadent flesh to fill his hands and were at the perfect angle for sucking. He palmed, squeezed and toyed with them until she squirmed, then he zeroed in on the puckered nubbins at the tips of those firm mounds and let his teeth have their wicked way. She'd always been partial to biting.

He lapped and nipped her beautiful breasts through her swimsuit while his fingers ran up and down toned, muscled calves and thighs, all on a five-foot-two frame. Chrysalyn was strong, compact and hippy, just the way he liked his women. Small package. Whole lot of beautiful female.

"Time to lose the swimsuit, Chrys," he groaned around

a succulent mouthful of her lovely areolas. Her stupefied "what" made him chuckle. He repeated his request, each word said with a little pluck to her nipples. She appeared ready to swoon.

"Chrysalyn, do you want me to stop?" he growled, backing off just enough to allow a cool stream of air to pass between their bodies. "Do you want me to stop, sweet?"

"Oh god, no!"

"Then. Remove. The. Suit."

With trembling fingers, she reached up and with a flick of her wrist undid the string secured around her neck. The top of her halter-style bikini fell free, revealing the tasty treats Rahn had been suckling through the fabric. And they were beautiful. Her breasts were full and firm, the color of caramel cappuccino with Hershey's Kisses nipples. Damn. With his chest wedged between her knees, he couldn't resist feasting a while longer and pulled the entire crown into his mouth while his fingers ducked into the warm flesh between her thighs.

There he found so much honeydew pleasure, he wanted to drown in her. The sounds echoing from her throat as he explored with lips, tongue and questing fingers were seductively sexy. But he wanted to push her over the edge, kick her ecstasy up a notch until she screamed to the heavens from now until the end of time.

Fingers slick with cream, he raised them up to her parted lips and pressed them inside.

"Taste yourself, love." Her tongue snaked out and wrapped around his finger, pulling and sucking until he felt the sensation clear down to his swollen balls. "God, woman, your scent is so sweet I can't wait another minute to sink my tongue into that pretty pussy."

She nodded dumbly, but didn't move, just sat there on the edge of the bubbling Jacuzzi, trembling as her chest heaved up and down. He would just have to be patient, because if he dared put his hands to her swimsuit bottom, it would be a shredded piece of no-good fabric when he was done yanking it off her succulent body. A succulent body with too many clothes on it!

Clenching his hands, he ground out, "Chrysalyn. The bottoms, sweet."

"Uh, yes. Okay." The words were breathy, lost. Hungry. And all for him.

She stood on the submerged seat and peeled the wet bottoms over the curve of her ass, down her lovely legs and dropped them on top of her sodden top on the deck. Settled again on the tub's edge, she spread her legs and flashed a siren's smile. The smoldering heat in her light brown eyes said come fuck me now. The engorged lips of her pussy, spread wide for him to see, screamed even louder. But no cock for her. Not yet.

He called quietly to his spirit guide one last time before he gorged himself on Chrysalyn's dewy folds.

'Mahpiya, lend me your senses.'

The reply was so faint, he almost missed it.

Take what I offer, my charge, and enjoy your mate. And then she faded away completely, leaving him and Chrysalyn truly alone.

Closing his eyes, he allowed the power and aura of the lioness to fill him until the very essence of his spirit guide whistled through every pore in his body. Then he lowered himself down into the water until only his chest was visible. The aroma of her sex, heightened by the lioness's keen senses, smelled of clean, fresh woman. And something else he couldn't quite pin down, like honey syrup and cardamom spice.

He kept his gaze pinned to hers as he pushed her thighs as far apart as they would go. The woman was practically doing the splits on the edge of that tub and he would take full advantage of it.

One swipe of his tongue up her dewy slit caused a strangled cry to erupt from between her lips.

"Oh dear god!"

A second pass brought on a shudder so intense, he thought she might keel over into the tub.

"Rahn! Oh, yesss!"

A third sent her spiraling toward release.

When the two of them had spent time together years ago, she'd never given him complete access to her body like this, saying she wanted to wait until the time was right. He'd been frustrated then, but now he was glad. This did feel, for lack of better words, right. Not forced or awkward. As if the pieces of their lives snapped together with perfect precision. The response to his touch was something he'd never dreamed of. It was as if he'd unwrapped a beautiful present, uncovered a rare jewel. And if her wild cries were any indication, the idiot she'd been engaged to had never gifted her with this kind of loving. Pride filled his chest as his lips and tongue continued to work her over.

"Oh god! Rahn! No more! I can't take it," she screamed. Mmm, what beautiful music. The cries torn from her throat as her orgasm peaked and consumed her filled his head as she exploded. The climax was forceful enough to set her slick channel clenching around the tip of his tongue and her legs trembling even while her knees wrapped tight around his head and her fingers gripped the edge of the tub.

Head thrown back, spine bowed, she gave herself up to his attention until she was a trembling mass of pliable flesh. Finally, Chrys collapsed backward onto the warm deck.

When her breathing returned to normal, she sat up and looked at him. What was that? Confusion? Fear? He couldn't tell.

The next instant, she snatched her wet swimsuit up off the deck and headed through the glass doors that led to her bedroom. The definitive snap and *click* told him she'd locked it behind her.

What the hell? Just as he started to go after her,

Mahpiya's powerful presence charged back into the familiar place in his head.

*Hoksila, *leave her be for now.**

Fuck.

'No worries, Mah. I can tell she needs a minute alone and so do I.'

His mate. Wow, he'd never expected such a thing. With that, Rahn climbed out of the tub and went back to his room. He flopped backward onto the bed, wrapped his fingers around his aching erection and closed his eyes. What would Chrysalyn's hot cunt feel like wrapped around him? Would she grip him tight? Would she yell like she'd done a few moments ago?

With his mind full of fantasy and his cock as hard as iron, he pulled and stroked himself until his balls drew up tight against his body. His come geysered onto his chest. The eruption provided scant relief, knowing he wouldn't be fully satisfied until he'd sunk into Chrysalyn's sweetness, binding her to him completely.

But why hadn't he realized this years ago? Mahpiya chimed in.

Because you were not ready to receive such a gift, hoksila. Certain events in your life have brought you to a place where you can appreciate her. Rest assured, Chrysalyn is the one.

'Thank you, Mah. Thanks for looking out for me.'

My pleasure and my duty, she whispered, retreating to her favorite corner with a yawn.

After a catnap, Rahn rose, showered again and headed to Chrysalyn's room. He was determined to win her, heart and soul. May as well start now.

It was still early enough, couldn't be much past ten a.m. Perhaps she would have breakfast with him?

"Chrys," he called quietly, tapping on her door.

No answer. Maybe she was napping as well?

"Chrys, love?"

Easing the door open, he was hit square in the chest by her scent, followed keenly by a disappointment so palpable he could have torn it in two and thrown it overboard. The room was empty. Chrys was gone.

CHAPTER FOUR

Over the years, he'd thought of Chrys often, but never contacted her out of respect. After all, she had someone else in her life, or he thought she had until this morning. But after tasting and touching the woman, after being in her presence again, he had to have her.

"Mahpiya, come to me," Rahn grumbled, deep in thought. He walked across the expanse of the living room and sat in the overstuffed chair directly across from Chrys' bedroom. His arm hung over the side of the linen-covered chair and was immediately propped up by the sleek back of an African female lion. Rahn's fingers automatically smoothed over the thick pelt, but stilled at Mahpiya's irritated growl.

May I remind you I am not one of your pathetic home cats.

"That's housecat, Mah," Rahn said with a grin. He knew where this conversation was going.

Whatever. She yawned with a muted roar. *I am queen of my domain and have no need of petting.*

Yep, she was proud all right. And beautiful and strong. But Rahn knew every woman needed a little stroking, no matter the species. "So, what if I need to do the petting? What if it soothes me? What then?"

If it is something you need, then I shall, of course, allow it. She sniffed and stretched her big body out on the plush carpet and Rahn buried his hand in her fur. Corded tendons and thick muscles bunched and twitched when his fingertips slipped over the spot just above her left shoulder. That was her sweet spot.

She rolled over on her side.

So why have you summoned me, my charge? the powerful spirit guide asked on a purr. Direct and to the point had always been her style. Rahn wished all females were this way. At least with Mahpiya, he always knew where he stood. If all was well, she said so. If he was being an idiot, Mahpiya had no bones about telling him. No second-guessing required.

"When I went to look for Chrys, she wasn't in her room. Is she running from me?"

Hoksila, you know I am not allowed to touch the thoughts of one who is not in my charge. I can only sense the emotions of others, however, with Chrysalyn I may be able to see somewhat deeper.

"Mah, what are you getting at?" Rahn asked, his eyebrows bunched in question.

If I answer your question, it would mean revealing a secret that is not mine.

With a frustrated sigh, Rahn pushed out of the chair and paced in front of the corporeal body of his guide before flopping back into the cushions.

"You can trust me, Mah. You know that."

Yes, I know, but I am not the one who must trust you. It is someone else.

"Chrys?"

In a manner of speaking.

"Is Chrys okay? Is everything all right?" He was no longer easing his hands along Mahpiya's back, but sat ramrod straight, brow knotted with tension. If something was wrong with Chrys, he wanted to know about it.

It is not what you think, hoksila. It is, in fact, a wondrous thing.

"Then tell me, before I go out of my mind with worry, damn it," he pressed. Rahn knew he was being less than polite with a female who tolerated no disrespect. But she did recognize that, while she was his spirit guide, he was all man. It was second nature to him to demand what was needed.

The lioness's tawny-eyed stare bore into his. Rahn couldn't have cared less.

"Tell me, Mah. Right this instant. What the hell is this secret that involves Chrys? You know I'm trustworthy, now out with it."

If you insist.

Seconds ticked by. Felt more like eons as they sat, holding each other's gaze. Suddenly, Mahpiya's expression softened, and she grinned as only a feline could.

I told you earlier Chrysalyn is your mate. What I did not tell you is that she has a spirit guide. An African lion, like me.

"What?" Rahn couldn't believe it. What were the odds of that? Of all the women he knew, the one he wanted more than anything had a spirit guide. But the realization raised more questions. If he and Chrys did get together, would the two spirit guides get along? Which one of the lionesses would lead their little pride? It was too amazing to conceive and sent his thoughts tumbling one over the other until they gelled enough to form a logical question.

"So what's her spirit guide's name?"

Adonei, Mahpiya said fondly. Rahn's brows rose. Well, it was obvious Mah already got along with the other lioness. Strange name, though.

"Adonei? What kind of a name is Adonei for a female?" he queried. At her response, his mouth fell wide open and practically hit the carpet.

Adonei is not a female. Adonei is a male, and he is my mate, as Chrysalyn is yours.

"You have got to be shitting me!"

Mates? Mah and this Adonei lion? Finally, his faithful companion would have someone especially for her. She was such a good guide, she deserved another who would love her, hunt with her and maybe even give her little spirit babies, if there was such a thing. Wait a minute. How did he know this Adonei was a good spirit? Sure, Mahpiya could sense such things, but they'd been together for years and he wouldn't just let anyone waltz into her life. After all, she deserved the best. Perhaps it was time for a little interview with Mr. Adonei.

"So," Rahn said evenly. "When can I expect to meet this Adonei?" Fingers steepled under his chin, the tips tapped together as he pinned Mahpiya with a glare. "If he's your mate, then as your only male relative, I demand to have a talk with him."

I appreciate your concern, hoksila. I love you as well.

"Mah," he growled impatiently when she didn't answer his question. She laughed! And when he was totally serious too!

You cannot speak directly with Adonei because you and Chrysalyn have not joined yet. But once your bond begins to form, you will be able to talk with him as easily as you speak with me. And there is more.

"Hell, Mah, I don't know if I can take any more news."

Adonei and I offer our assistance in securing your mate.

"Huh?" he asked as his mind tried to wrap around what his spirit guide said.

I said, we wish to help you win Chrysalyn.

Boy, this just got better and better. He felt an idiotic grin spread across his lips, but couldn't seem to control his facial muscles.

If you want her, that is.

"Of course I want her. I've always wanted her. What man in his right mind wouldn't want a woman like Chrys?" Regret had been his constant companion since he'd blown his first chance with Chrys. The woman evoked such strong feelings in him, she was the only female he knew who made him feel so...unsteady. But like a fool, he'd allowed himself to be distracted by other things. By the time he'd figured out she was everything he'd ever wanted in a woman, she was engaged to what's-his-butt.

So what happened between the two of them? Why hadn't they gotten married?

I know you have questions, but until Chrysalyn accepts you, spirit, soul and body, you must speak to Adonei through me. I will do my best to ensure we communicate well.

"Thanks, Mah. I love you, you know that, you big beautiful cat?"

Big cat? Humph!

"Okay, you and Adonei fill me in." A noticeable pep in his step, Rahn made his way to the kitchen, listening to Mah's sultry voice. All this news about mates and spirit guides made him hungry. Not to mention the wonderfully intimate time he'd spent with Chrys early this morning.

After a bit of rummaging around, he found everything he needed to make a nutritious brunch. Slicing a sushi-grade filet of Ahi tuna, Rahn made a quick dish of Hawaiian poké, complete with fresh ginger, spicy soy sauce, fragrant green onions and a dash of sesame oil served up on a bed of crisp lettuce. He sat down at the dining room table, picked up a single bite of the delicacy and froze with his fork in midair.

Suddenly uncomfortable, his eyes immediately scanned the area for the source of the sensation, but it seemed to come from far off and was unfamiliar as it flowed down the psychic bond he shared with his spirit guide. His skin felt stretched tight and almost itchy. His gut churned until it felt pulled inside out. An air of deep disgust settled in, so strong he wanted to rip off his t-shirt and jeans, run back to the shower and scrub until he felt clean again.

"Mah, what the hell's going on? What's wrong?"

It is not me, my charge. Adonei is uneasy with the company Chrysalyn is keeping.

"Show me." Understanding dawned the second he closed his eyes and Adonei shared the situation with Mahpiya, who then shared it with Rahn. A lovely image of

Chrys filled his mind, so clear he could see each individual strand of her short wavy hair. Her cocoa skin was so flawless, it reminded him of a smooth river of milk chocolate. And he'd learned this morning that it was just as sweet. The need to touch her almost overwhelmed. But if he reached out, could he brush his fingers over the curve of her shoulder?

Then the vision shifted and the hair on the back of Rahn's neck stood at full attention. He didn't hear his fork clatter into his plate, then down to the tiled floor. A burst of adrenaline hit his bloodstream. The urge to take off at a dead run had him clenching his leg muscles as Mah sent the unfolding situation into his mind. He wasn't sure he'd ever felt such apprehension, even when pursuing the nastiest of villains. And these feelings came from Chrysalyn's spirit guide through Mahpiya? And so strong?

He was out the door in two shakes.

Once on the elevator, he wished he'd taken the stairs. The damned thing was moving too slow. Surely he could have run faster than this. The thoughts flowing into his mind gave a whole new meaning to the phrase slower than molasses.

Damn, he had to get a hold of himself. Dealing with the thoughts of three entities—Mahpiya, Adonei and himself—he'd be so worked up by the time he got to Chrys, he'd simply deck the man who was causing such concern. Then he'd toss Chrys over his shoulder and carry her back to their apartment, caveman style.

The idea had merit, but it would certainly bring more attention than he wanted. Before he could say anything, Mahpiya once again proved why she was the spirit guide and he was her charge. The cat was one step ahead of him, as usual.

I must cease sharing Adonei's concern with you. We do not wish for you to behave irrationally when you arrive at your destination. Adonei and I wish to assist you in winning Chrysalyn, not make her angry.

Thankful for the calm reassurance, Rahn took a deep breath and stilled himself.

'Thanks, Mah,' he whispered along their bond as the elevator doors opened with a quiet swish. 'I'll call if I need you, but before you stand down, ask Adonei one more question for me.'

Yes?

'The name of the man with Chrys.'

Adonei says his name is Eden Pall. They met shortly after Chrys boarded a few days ago. Something about him simply does not smell right to Adonei.

'Thanks, Mah. You can stand down now.'

As you wish, she whispered, retreating to the special little corner of his mind where she liked to nap.

Slowing his stride, he made his way into the restaurant. One look at Chrys' beautiful self and his tongue stuck to the roof of his mouth. The woman was dressed in a formfitting sports bra and matching cropped workout pants. All curves and luscious skin, yet she screamed strength and ability. Damn, even her tennis shoes looked sexy. A glance at the man with whom she kept company stripped the slight smile from his face. His jaw began to hurt. Well, no wonder—he was grinding his teeth. The Eden fellow sat looking like he wanted to eat her up along with whatever he had on his breakfast plate. But not today. Or any other day, for that matter.

The second she spotted Rahn making a beeline for her table, she looked like a deer in the headlights. He hoped she'd close her mouth before something flew into it. But as for the dark look he received from her temporary partner, Rahn had seen it before, and always on someone up to no good. Oh yeah, that's just what he was looking for and would make sure to call his boss, Geri, today to check this guy out. The man looked normal enough, but the veneer was too smooth. His pasted-on smile, too perfect. This guy was bad news. Rahn felt it down in his gut and, obviously, Chrys' spirit guide did too. So why was she here? If Adonei had sent even half of what he'd shared with Mahpiya down his psychic link with Chrys, how in the world could she sit here looking so calm?

Rahn strolled right up to the couple, ignored the encroacher and leaned down to plant a kiss just at the corner of Chrys' decadently tempting mouth.

"Hello, love. When I awoke, you were gone. I missed you. Everything all right?"

* * * * *

God, if Adonei didn't quiet down, she was going to go bonkers. His displeasure at Eden popping up to share her brunch was beyond palpable. The lion's anger and agitation, like the scraping of sharp claws across a chalkboard, filled the inside of her skull. Chrys' teeth were set on edge and had her more than ready to plead a very real headache and flee the table. Something about her present company rubbed Adonei completely the wrong way.

Head down, pretending to study the breakfast menu, Chrys tried to get Adonei to talk to her. Her churning stomach made her queasy. Something made Adonei's skin crawl. She felt it through the bond, as if a dark and demented presence traipsed a slimy finger up her arm leaving goose bumps in its wake. Oh god, she was going to be sick. Had she remembered to pack her migraine medicine? She sure as hell hoped so. And she couldn't get mad at Adonei. He wasn't trying to hurt her, but whatever had him ready to pounce swooshed down their psychic link and slammed into her mind like the pounding of waves against the sand in the middle of a storm.

"Chrysalyn, you seem ill."

Eden's thick accent was exotically sexy in her ears, but slid over her soul like rancid oil. When her company reached over and gently covered her hand with his, the sick swirl in her belly intensified and sweat broke out on her top lip.

She eased her hand from underneath his, swallowed the

bile racing into her mouth and picked up the glass sitting in front of her. Chrys didn't think she'd ever been so happy to see iced water in her life. Even the condensation dripping down the side of the crystal goblet called her name, invited her to cool the suddenly feverish skin on the inside of her palm.

God, the liquid felt so good sliding down her throat to calm her stomach.

"Chrysalyn, are you all right?" Eden asked again.

"Uh, sure, I'm fine," she sputtered and forced a smile while waving down the waiter. She placed her order and then took another sip of water, followed by shallow breaths. Out of the corner of her eye, she caught sight of a tall, wide figure moving her way with a determined posture. The man, intimidating body language and all, wasn't a danger to her. If he were, Adonei would have put up even more racket than he had since Eden sat down a few moments ago. God, and those moments felt like eternity.

Suddenly, Adonei went still. He continued to pad back and forth across the forefront of her mind, but other than that there wasn't a single roar. Not even a sniff or a yawn. And her nausea, headache, goose bumps and shivering disappeared as if they'd never been. Strange.

She turned and locked gazes with one of the most beautiful men she'd ever known. Rahn. The second their eyes met, Chrys could have sworn she felt a light brush of relief against her thoughts from her spirit guide.

His long legs ate up the distance between them as he approached, all brawn, class and a nice tight ass. Oh, goodness, had she really thought up a poem in honor of Rahn's backside? An unusual tightness encircled her tongue as she watched him come. Resisting the urge to roll her eyes at her own goofy line of thinking, she snapped closed the mouth she hadn't realized was wide open. A heated blush crept up her neck.

Rahn's dark hair, though tastefully cut, was slightly

mussed, as if he'd taken a shower, dressed quickly and come straight to her. The sexy smirk that had always made her knees tremble was firmly in place. And the gleam in his golden brown eyes screamed to the world that he wanted nothing more than to get next to her.

There was no subtlety about his intent as he stepped to her side. A soft musky scent filled the scant space between them. God, he smelled good. Looked good. Felt good. Licked and sucked good.

She squeezed her eyes shut and tried to push the thoughts away. She couldn't sit here with Eden and think about how deliciously Rahn had feasted on her still-throbbing pussy just after sunrise. It just wasn't right. Chrys didn't like Eden *that way*, but it felt naughty to think on such intimate details in the presence of another man.

And Rahn wasn't making it easy on her. Especially when he leaned forward, his breath tickling her ear just before he dropped a kiss dangerously close to her lips. Her mouth almost fell open again when he started talking about how much he'd missed her when he woke to find her gone. And the man made no attempt to keep his voice down, either. Damn it, he'd have everyone thinking they were sleeping together! They were in the same apartment, but they weren't sleeping together. Hot-tubbing maybe, but definitely not sleeping, though the idea was beginning to have merit.

God, she was really losing it.

Rahn eased into a pub chair. His thigh brushed against hers as he reached across the table and extended a friendly hand to Eden. A glance at her tablemate stilled the blood in her heart. She almost called his name to see if she could snap him out of his...whatever he was in. Lips set in a stern line, Eden didn't move, didn't blink, showed no expression at all. The man looked as if he were carved from stone.

"Hello," Rahn said in as friendly a tone as she'd ever heard. "I'm Rahn. Traveling with Chrys for, ah, work."

The urge to kick him in the shin when he turned and winked at her almost overrode her common sense. There was no missing the implication as the knowing smirk reappeared, accompanied by a slyly arched brow. How did he pull that off without looking like a smart-ass? And now that he was seated next to her, his presence swirled around her, reached for her. Focusing on her spirit guide, she was surprised to find Adonei settled down, watching the byplay. The big cat had ceased pacing and now sat on his huge haunches, watching curiously to see what would happen between the two males sharing her table.

Hmm. What was going on here?

'Adonei, is there something I should know? You're awfully calm all of a sudden,' she whispered in her mind, sneaking another peek at Rahn from underneath her lashes. Geesh, the man was gorgeous even when he ordered coffee. And if the big grin spread across the face of the perky little waitress was any indication, Chrys wasn't the only one who thought so.

A bagel and cream cheese was hustled to the table along with a small bowl full of sweet, sliced melon. Chrys found her eyes glued to the sinewy play of muscle in Rahn's forearm. Skilled fingers moved gracefully as he spread some strawberry cream cheese over the toasted bread. The lightly tanned skin exposed by his dark blue three-quarter-sleeved t-shirt was smooth, but heavily veined and stretched over thick ropy tendons. The bulge of biceps pushed against the fabric, hinting at the raw power of his honed body. Damn, he was sexy.

And could have anyone he wanted. So what the hell did he want with her? The answer lit her mind like a beacon.

Chrys sniffed and turned away. She was nobody's fool. Rahn may have alluded that he was more to her than a coworker, but he was just posturing because Eden was there. Typical male. He might not want her, but he didn't want anyone else to have her either. So what about the stint in the hot tub? Again, typical male. What man could resist a half naked woman in a hot tub?

Here we go, she thought with a silent snort. *Two men all cocksure over a woman neither of them have any right to.*

Eden hadn't gotten anywhere near being intimate with her. And Rahn obviously thought a few perfectly placed licks of his talented tongue meant he could pick up with her where they'd left off three years ago. Now that pissed her off.

Besides, their previous estrangement was all his fault. He was the one who'd decided to get so wrapped up in his cases that he didn't have time for her. And he sure as hell gave no indication he'd intended to ask for her hand while getting himself caught up in the agency's floozy of the year. So Chrys had cut her losses and moved on. Shortly after she'd become engaged to Sean, Rahn had moved back to London and pretty much disappeared from her life. All she knew was he occasionally worked out of the Miami, London and Rome offices. He'd only tried to contact her once since then.

On a trip back to Denver, he'd managed to get her alone in the office for a minute. He'd wanted her back. But, hell, at the time she'd been too busy trying to figure out what was going on with the idiot she was engaged to.

Yep, she'd picked an insensitive blockhead to get over Rahn and ended up cutting off her nose to spite her face. It wasn't something she'd advertised after the wedding was called off. In fact, no one except her cousin, Delaine, and her boss, Geri, had even known the real deal until almost six months past the wedding that never happened.

So what was Rahn really doing here? Was it just work? His possessive overtures and attempt to seduce her—an attempt that was working quite well until a few seconds ago, by the way—said it was nothing more than just an investigation in Rome. But if he needed to get somewhere, why take the long way 'round on a cruise ship with her?

Her suspicion grew as she watched him. The smile plastered on Rahn's face certainly didn't reach his eyes. In fact, she couldn't recall spotting such a cold, calculating look on the man.

And now that she was really paying attention, Eden got more and more fidgety the longer he sat in Rahn's presence. So what was Eden's problem? He'd practically come right out and said he was interested in her. Now that Rahn appeared, he was just going to up and back off? Now she was really annoyed.

'Adonei, come to me,' Chrysalyn called across their bond. The fully mature lion rose and stalked forward until his image practically filled the very forefront of her mind.

'Adonei, what is going on with Rahn? He's being civil enough, but he seems to be feeling Eden out like he'd do with a suspect on one of his cases.'

He has every right to be protective of you, Chrysalyn, Adonei said quietly, seriously.

'Really? Why is that?' she snarled sarcastically along their link.

He is your mate.

A sip of coffee slipped down the wrong pipe into her lungs. "Oh please!" she hacked around rough racking coughs. Oops, she hadn't meant to say that out loud.

Rahn's head snapped around and his golden brown gaze captured hers. No mask. No schooled features. No pretense. Only true and genuine concern was mirrored there.

He reached out a hand and covered hers gently. "What was that, Chrys? What's wrong, love?" His words were pitched low in his throat with a smooth and inviting timbre, laced with care. Bastard.

Before she could answer, Eden wiped his mouth on a crisp linen napkin and tossed it gracefully onto the table next to his half empty plate.

Chrys frowned as she watched him tidy up his area as if he were leaving. What the hell did Eden have to be uncomfortable about? She was the one sharing an apartment with the most striking man in all of creation.

And that damned English accent of his made her body shiver until she clenched her thighs together to keep from coming in her fitness pants. And she wasn't supposed to want him, damn it! Eden was a welcome distraction, damn it.

"If you'll excuse me, Ms. Geyer."

She schooled her features, wanting nothing more than to snap her neck to the side and settle her fist on her hip. Ms. Geyer? What happened to calling her Chrysalyn?

Eden rose smoothly to his feet. "I believe I shall go and see about arranging a tour for our next port of call. Perhaps we can finish our conversation later?"

And now her welcome distraction extracted himself from her presence. Sigh. Maybe she could still salvage the situation? She smiled and opened her mouth to agree, but Rahn cut her off.

"You know, love," he crooned, turning to her. "I was thinking perhaps we could take a private tour of Ibiza when we get to the Balearic Islands. One of the owners brought along a few toys, including a jet boat. You game, Chrys?"

Raising a hand in the universal I surrender gesture, Eden gave a slight bow and left as quickly as he'd appeared.

Rahn grinned like a rogue. God, she wanted to smack the cocky grin off his face. Besides, he had no intention of taking her anywhere. He was just trying to head off Eden. Damned man.

With schooled features and a plastic smile of her own, she eased her plate back and away, along with the coffee she hadn't finished.

"You arrogant, self-centered, son of a…"

"What? What'd I do?" Rahn asked with wide-eyed innocence. If she'd been a novice she would have actually believed the sinless-as-an-angel reaction. Out of her seat, she stilled when he swiveled around in his chair and wrapped his fingers firmly around her biceps, preventing her from leaving.

"Where are you going?"

"Last I checked, I was on vacation and not reporting to anyone. Not even our boss," she growled quietly, not wanting to draw attention to their little quarrel in the middle of a packed eatery. Especially since the restaurant was on-board ship and she'd surely have to see at least some of these people again.

"Chrys, baby, don't be mad."

"Don't be mad? I'm stuck on this damned floating palace for three months and you just chased away my potential hang-out buddy. Now what the hell am I supposed to do? Just sit around with my thumb up my ass, bored out of my head?"

"Sweetheart…"

"Don't you dare sweetheart me, Rahn."

"Chrys, I meant what I said. I do want to spend time with you, and I really did look into some private tours for us. Just last night, actually, right after I came aboard."

"Wha…?"

"When I joined you in the hot tub this morning, it wasn't meant to be a one-time event."

He pulled her closer until she stood between his long legs. Aw, hell, her insides were going all gooey. *Come on, girlfriend, snap that spine in place.* Hmmm, the spine wasn't listening. Just great.

"I intend to make up for all the time I spent without you."

"Oh, be real, Rahn. You were just postulating, doing the mark-my-territory thing."

"You want me to be honest, Chrys?"

"Yes, damn it." She almost lost her train of thought when he took both her hands in his and kissed each knuckle. The heat of his inner thighs burned through the fabric of her workout pants and scalded her legs where they connected with his knees.

"Here's real for you, love. I plan to seduce you. And

most importantly, I plan to keep you. Period."

CHAPTER FIVE

He released her hands and slowly eased his strong arms around her waist. His gaze was hot, unwavering as he slowly eased her even closer. Oh god, he was going to kiss her right here in the restaurant! Her stomach danced wildly, and like a puppet on a string, her feet followed his direction without her permission. Her lips tingled in anticipation of feeling his mouth on hers, his wide solid chest pressed against hers. Oh, dear god. She had to go right now. Either that or melt into the glossy varnish of the hardwood floors.

She pushed away.

"Chrys?" he asked, his voice full of what she could only describe as expectancy. And not only did she know what he wanted, she actually wanted to give it to him. What the hell?

"I'm going to the spa, Rahn. Alone."

"Fine. I'll walk you to the elevator."

"Rahn, I don't need…"

But he was already out of his seat, guiding her through the fancy glass double doors and toward the elevator with a hand at the small of her back.

He steered her into a little nook she hadn't noticed on

her way into the restaurant. The second her body disappeared into the shadows, his big body blocked out the rest of the light as he swooped in for the kiss she hadn't allowed at the table. And, lord, could he kiss.

She tried to resist, but after a few seconds of deliciously intimate nibbling, the quiet moan locked in her throat slipped through. Then Chrys let him take her very breath away. His lips were insistent as they moved over hers. His earthy male scent mixed with the chocolate mocha coffee he'd been drinking and stole her very senses. Her body arched into his and earned a ragged groan as his rapidly swelling cock pressed against her belly. He held her so tight. How wonderful to be engulfed in his embrace, held so securely against his honed body.

It felt good to know she was the cause of the flex and ripple of muscle under her fingers. His pecs and abs tightened and fluttered as she explored his body through the kiss.

Reluctant to come up for air, Chrys let one of her hands slip up the side of his neck and bury itself in his thick, silky hair. She almost tightened her grip to the scalp and pulled him back to her mouth when he eased away.

"Chrys, baby, I've missed you so much. I don't know if this is the right time, but I've got to tell you this."

Suddenly, apprehension bit at the base of her spine. What was he going to say? Had he changed his mind about his intention to seduce her? Considering the fact they'd been estranged until just last night, should she be surprised if he walked away?

Then her spirit guide, without her having to ask, sent reassuring care and love through their bond and she instantly relaxed. What did Adonei know that she didn't? She'd have to have a long talk with that damned lion as soon as she got some time to herself.

"Chrys, listen, I know I practically disappeared after you got engaged to what's-his-name." The way he spit out what's-his-name made her smile. "But I've never stopped caring for you. Wanting you. The only reason I asked for a transfer to London was because I couldn't stand to see you with someone else. I still can't."

He leaned down, pressed his forehead against hers and waited.

"So," she said on a sigh as his hands gently caressed the tense muscles of her lower back. "What do you want, Rahn?"

"I want you, love."

She went still as stone. Now why hadn't she expected such an answer? Because she hadn't believed anything he'd said this morning. And now she felt caught in the headlights. It had never been a feeling she enjoyed, whether the situation was good or not.

But, damn it, if she was going to be a deer in the headlights, Chrysalyn Geyer wasn't going to stand in traffic alone. Her hands dropped away from his chest as she tried to create some space between them. She would have succeeded except for the wall at her back.

"Why are you really here, Rahn? Is it because you have a murder to investigate, a case to solve? Are you here for work or for me?"

He gritted his teeth and hesitated. And she had her answer.

"Bye, Rahn."

"Damn, it, woman."

Squeezing past him, she'd made it almost a whole foot away when she was snatched back against a wall of a rock-hard chest. Then the marvelously muscular man planted a sweet peck on her cheek.

"You know I can't tell you. But I will say I've learned from losing you the first time. Work will never take your place. Not this time, love." He kissed her again, this time so gently she felt tears gather behind her eyes. She pushed him back with a deep, though purposely annoyed-sounding, intake of breath.

"Check in with me after you're done at the spa."

She started. He held up his hand in a conciliatory gesture and continued. "I know you can take care of yourself, but I mean it, Chrys. Be careful off by yourself." This followed by a ground-out "Please", before he strode away.

Gaze glued to his retreating back, Chrys allowed herself a moment to admire his ass. Damn, he looked good in jeans. A lopsided grin tipped up one side of her mouth as she stepped inside the elevator.

Reaching out to her spirit guide, Chrys called to the big cat.

'Adonei, did you catch that?'

Of course. It is my task to look after you, is it not?

'Well, yeah, but it looks like you might have to fight Rahn for the job. By the way, you've never been so silent while I was in the company of a man lately. Only with Rahn.'

He is your mate. It is only right to give him that respect.

'Mate, eh? But why now? Why not years ago?' Maybe the knowledge would have kept both of them from making stupid mistakes.

Because neither of you were ready to accept what you meant to each other then. Hence, it was not made known to me the importance of this human male.

'And we are now? Ready, I mean?' she asked with a snort and a grin.

It would seem so, yes.

'Well, mate or not, if he thinks he's gonna start ordering me around, he's got another think coming.'

The elevator stopped and slid silently open. Chrys stepped out and her mouth, which seemed to be falling open often these days, made the trip again. The entrance to the opulent spa was a set of wide gold and glass doors with Clinique La Paris written in elegant frosted script across the panes. A massage, manicure and pedicure awaited her, but thoughts of the interactions with Rahn intruded. That, along with Adonei's words, ran rampant through her brain. Mate. Mate. Mate?

It was useless to try to hide the chemistry with Rahn, especially when her body responded so eagerly to his touch. Not to mention he was genuinely a good guy. Hell, who was she kidding? If there was a word for beyond attracted, it would almost sum up her feelings for the man.

She checked in with the technician and was shown to a plush private room to change. Her toes wiggled as the warmth from the heated tile eased into the soles of her feet. It was so soothing, she was almost reluctant to climb up on the massage table and pull the sheet over her naked body. Her mind strayed to Rahn again, to the desire she saw in his eyes when he looked at her, the softness with which he touched her. The fierceness of his loving as he took her with lips, teeth and tongue. Immediately, her nipples tingled and soon stabbed into the warm blanket she lay on.

Three months of vacation, eh? But that was her predicament, not his. He was, after all, working on a case. Would he rejoin her on the ship after he wrapped up his investigation in Rome, or simply fly home alone? She had no idea, but she had the whole crossing of the Mediterranean before she had to worry about it. If she played her cards right, at least some of her too-long trip would be interesting. If she could just manage to keep a little part of herself from falling.

* * * * *

Eden took the elevator up to his sprawling apartment. Ignoring the call of both the pharaoh and her charges, he whipped off his day clothes, neatly folded the cargo pants and t-shirt and left them on top of the washing machine. He strode to the master bedroom and yanked on his customary all-black hunting garb, then changed his mind. Where he was going, the slacks and silk shirt would stand out. He opted for a black sweatsuit instead and was out the door in less than five minutes.

In the fitness area, he walked around the large wide-open rooms. Finally, Eden spotted a woman who fit the description of the last one he'd been instructed to correct. As he followed her from the fitness area to the indoor pool, he sighed inwardly. The female didn't exude any apprehension or concern. In fact, she didn't seem to notice being followed at all. No thrill to the hunt. No exhilaration or surge of energy as on other forays. Strange.

"This is fucking boring," he mumbled to himself. His steps were silent, but he'd spoken too loudly and caused the specimen to turn around and look behind her. Damn it. He knelt and pretended to tie his shoelace.

He waited for his pharaoh to speak to him while surveying the occupants. Nothing. No hints or clues as to who he was supposed to exact justice upon. Now he wished he'd taken a moment to answer her when she'd called to him while he changed his clothes.

But that damned hybrid infidel who'd practically accosted Chrysalyn at the breakfast table had him charged up and wired for sound. Seething didn't come close to describing his agitation.

He chastised himself while resisting the urge to roll his eyes toward the ceiling. "Get your mind into the game, Eden." But his brain wouldn't cooperate. It kept turning back toward the beautiful and exotic Chrysalyn.

Their time together at breakfast had been pleasant until her big coworker showed up. Chrysalyn seemed completely comfortable with the man. If Eden wasn't mistaken, the fellow appeared to be of Egyptian birth. But no, his skin was too light, his speech too Western. But he couldn't take the chance that this Rahn person came from the same homeland. If the bastard was indeed a kinsman and saw Eden acquiring Chrysalyn the way he intended to, his plans would be foiled. He'd become an outcast.

For the first time in ten years of cleansing the world of the unworthy, Eden was nervous. A bizarre and unwelcome sensation. Why was this happening to him, and why now?

He let his intended prey go on alone and sat down on one of the cushioned seats along the hallway. Quieting his mind he called out to his pharaoh. Again, nothing. The voice of his devoted pharaoh and harem keeper did not penetrate the morass of confusion that assailed him. No spiritual awareness. No voice in his head. Just a big black void.

Inwardly, his heart pounded at the prospect of something having happened to his beloved tarot reader. Never one to bring unnecessary attention to himself, Eden forced his feet to take calm, measured steps back to his apartment. Suddenly a thought flashed into the forefront of his mind. The Empress. The apprehension grew. He had to know what the hell was going on with that damned card.

Eden stepped over the threshold into his foyer. Once inside, he pulled a deep cleansing breath into his lungs and let it whoosh out. Again, in and out. The third time around, he finally felt the tension begin to leach from his limbs and relaxation take its place. His harem keeper was where he'd left her. All was well.

Beloved, what is wrong? You are tense?

Eden removed his shoes at the door, strode to her case and gently removed her from the shelf.

"I needed you while I was on the hunt and you did not respond. I did not like it."

But, beloved, I never accompany you on the hunt. We always speak before you depart…

Yes, damn it, he knew that. But this time he'd needed her, needed her presence in his head. Who the hell cared what she always did or didn't do? The only thing that mattered was right here and now.

Easing down into his favorite oversized chair near the coffee table, Eden set his harem keeper down on the coffee table, picked up the black and gold tarot deck he kept there and shuffled it.

The Empress. Upside down.

Again, he shuffled, yet drew the same card.

Last time he'd asked about this card, his lovely pharaoh blew him off. Not this time.

"I want to know what this fucking card means and right now."

She remained quiet a moment. Eden knew she was preparing some kind of bullshit answer, but he wasn't going for it. His gut churned. Sweat erupted from his brow and crept down the side of his face, dampening the skin all the way down to his neck. He had a feeling Chrysalyn might be affected by this particular draw as well as himself.

"Tell me what this card means or you will find yourself in need of an heir to take up your rule."

Snapping her lovely brown porcelain neck was no hardship for him. He'd simply have another made. Or better yet, allow one of her charges to take her place. They were growing tired of her heavy-handed tactics anyway.

Beloved, there is no need to be angry. I do not believe you have selected this card for you, but for someone else. Someone you will meet or have recently encountered.

"Just tell me what the fuck it means," he growled. His nostrils flared as the tip of his nose smashed against her dainty little porcelain one. Then silence. Finally, she spoke, though her exasperated tone made him feel more like a scolded little boy than her master. Fine, he'd deal with it later.

As a man, it indicates the weakening of the figure of your beloved, either because you are experiencing your feelings and sentiments less intensely, or the woman is losing love because she is physically or emotionally distant. That is all.

Her voice trailed off.

Eden leaned his head against the backrest of the chair. With understanding came relief and the knots in his stomach loosened. It was so clear to him now. The man who wanted Chrysalyn, the Rahn asshole, was losing her. The woman was losing love for him. She must be coming to realize how good she and Eden would be together.

After all, she did appear to be a smart female.

With a bit more pep in his step, Eden kissed his harem keeper on the very forehead he'd been ready to smash moments before. Setting her back in her case, he touched his fingers to his lips and blew her a kiss, not bothering to hide a grin.

Yes, she would have to be destroyed. He simply couldn't have his little taskmaster trying to make Chrysalyn's life difficult once they got together.

And get together, they would.

CHAPTER SIX

Rahn paid a courtesy visit to the ship's captain, Todd Laurens. Thankfully, the shrewd and experienced man was more than pleased to have a discreetly armed and qualified agent on board. After dismissing the lower-ranking officers from the bridge, Captain Laurens and his First Officer, Lt. Spans, offered to provide any assistance Rahn needed. He'd been ordered to keep a tight wrap on the details of the case and they were all on the same page. The captain and the government of the ship's origin wanted nothing more than to keep it quiet that this vessel might be connected to a string of grisly murders spanning the Mediterranean and beyond.

After the brief meeting, he returned to the apartment he shared with Chrys, had a quick lunch, then scouted the ship from top to bottom. He noticed nothing out of the ordinary, but Mahpiya's constant growling in the back of his mind let him know something was more than wrong.

The sun was setting by the time he made it back to the spacious suites. Damn it, Chrys wasn't back yet. And there was no message on the voice mail from her, either.

Rahn prowled from one end of the huge apartment to the other. Through the living room and dining room, into the kitchen and back. The next trip took him from his bedroom, out the sliding glass doors onto the deck and into Chrys' room. Her enticing spiced ginger scent was everywhere. He stood next to her oversized bed and couldn't resist reaching down to grab one of her pillows. Face buried in the center of it, he inhaled deeply, drew her rich, womanly scent into his lungs.

The smell brought the memory of how perfectly her thighs cradled his head while he lapped at her succulent pussy. How her soft moans wrapped around his cock and squeezed relentlessly. The honeyed taste of the soft skin of her lips, the curve of her neck and her breasts with their chocolate cherry nipples. His fingers itched to bury themselves in the cottony down of her hair and pull her lush, inviting mouth against his. Wanted to feel her sharp teeth nibble and nip all of his sensitive areas as she explored his body.

She was such a beautiful female. All dark skin, light brown eyes and short midnight silky hair. He wished she'd let it grow out to its former length so he could wrap it around his hands while he rode her from behind. Chrys was a succulent treat, like syrup dribbled over cinnamon ice cream. And she was his. His woman. His damned stubborn woman who hadn't bothered to let him know where she was all day.

He tossed the pillow haphazardly into the center of her bed and stomped back to the kitchen. He hit the speakerphone button on the satellite phone hanging on the wall, punched in a number and listened to the line ring while he pulled out the bowl of leftover poké.

His boss picked up the phone and Rahn confirmed their worst suspicions. Each of the murders had indeed occurred in a port of call right before this particular ship departed for its next destination. And it was getting more and more difficult to keep the information from leaking out to the public.

"So what do you have?" Geri asked. Her fingernails

click, click, clicked on her computer keyboard in the background.

"Captain Laurens wants to accompany me into town at the next port. I'm having a hard time convincing him not to get involved. I wish you'd warned me he's a former Navy man. Getting him to stay out of this is proving difficult," he said around a mouthful of food. It was quickly washed down with a swig of iced tea.

"Is difficult? Does that mean you haven't succeeded?"

"Hardly. I reminded him that our agency's survival depends on our ability to remain secret. Blend in with the populace. I pointed out that it would be strange for him, a man who's sure to be recognized by both crew and passengers, to be seen with me in the seedier parts of each town."

"Didn't work, eh?"

"Not even close. *He* reminded *me* that nothing about the victims or the places they were found was seedy. Still, only he and his first officer know why I'm here."

"And what about Chrys?"

"I told her I'm investigating a case in Rome."

"And she bought it?" Geri asked with disbelief.

"Doubt it. She's a smart woman. I'm sure she's already figured that if I needed to be in Rome for something important, I'd be there by now, and not tooling through the Mediterranean on a luxury cruise ship."

"Any leads?"

"Nothing other than a few vague descriptions of a possible suspect," Rahn reported. "But something odd is going on, something off. I can feel it. By the way, there's someone I want you to check out for me. A man named Eden Pall. Five foot, ten inches. About a hundred and seventy pounds. I'm not sure where he's from, but he looks and sounds of Egyptian descent."

"Egyptian? Why don't you use your own contacts to run him down?"

"I already put a call in to my aunt. She's working on it.

I'd already planned to stay a couple of days at her house in Alexandria when we pull into port, anyway. She'll have something for me by the time we get there."

One of the advantages of having a family full of law enforcement specialists. Whether at home in England or Egypt, there was the benefit of contacts who happened to be relatives.

Finished with his snack, he set the bowl in the sink and rinsed it quickly.

"Geri, I'd still like you to pull a report on him. It couldn't hurt. And it'll be days before we get to Egypt and Aunt Suman won't call me on board, no matter what. It would be just my luck that Chrys would answer the phone. My aunt never could lie to Chrys."

Geri's "uh-huh" of agreement was quickly followed by a nosy, "Any chance you and Chrys might hook up?"

"Speaking of hook up," Rahn deliberately blew her off. "What happened to Chrys and what's-his-name? Why didn't they get married?"

"Well, I'm not sure if I should tell you this, but knowing Chrys, she probably won't spill it." Geri paused, sounding a bit uncomfortable with the subject. Rumor had it his boss felt personally responsible for Chrys' unhappiness. "You know I introduced her to Sean, right? After she decided you would never ask her to marry you, I was just trying to help her move on. He'd held some of the highest positions on the Department of Justice payroll. And now we know why. The man was an expert at keeping secrets, especially his own."

"What are you getting at?" Rahn asked impatiently. Fingers raked a path through his hair as he snatched the phone off the hook, put it to his ear and paced. The carpet on the living room floor was so spongy and thick underneath his boots that he left tracks. He hated leaving tracks. Geri continued.

"Well, Chrys found out he had a whole 'nother family right here in Denver. She'd met a young boy named Alex, who Sean introduced as his son. Chrys thought it was just some kind of 'Big Brothers-Big Sisters' thing. After all, Sean is white as the driven snow and Alex is African American, like Chrys. Turned out Sean was married to the boy's mother and had been keeping Chrys a secret. Not to mention Chrys would have been wife number four, which he'd also neglected to mention, though she'd asked him flat out how many times he'd been married. Hell, if he couldn't be honest, hid a wife, a son and a daughter, and couldn't stay married after three tries, Chrys certainly didn't want to get saddled with someone like that. Especially not at twenty-five years old. So, she canceled the wedding and cut him off."

"So, did you cut his balls off slowly, or in one quick swipe?" Rahn asked, bristling at the thought of someone hurting Chrys in such a callous way. Bastard. Perhaps Rahn would look him up when he got back to the States.

"I don't know how, but we managed to keep it quiet. There would have been plenty of agents upset about the way it all went down. They all love Chrys. Of course, she threatened to 'disappear' both me and Delaine if we touched Sean. She just wanted it to all go away, so she simply pushed it to the back of her mind and threw herself into her work. She's been working herself to the bone ever since, which is why I forced her to take this vacation."

"About this vacation, Eden Pall is supposedly taking a holiday. But he's a bit too interested in Chrys."

And speaking of Chrys, where the hell was the woman?

Mahpiya's voice slipped into his mind. *She is near.*

'Near and here are two different things. I told her to check in with me, damn it. Doesn't she know it's dangerous?'

Chrysalyn senses an odd darkness in the spirit realm, but cannot determine whether it is focused on her or not, so no, she does not realize it is dangerous. She returned here after her spa treatment, but it was during the time you spoke with the leader of this vessel.

Rahn's attitude instantly reduced from an angry

tyrannosaurus rampage down to miffed male seethe. At least Chrys wasn't avoiding him. Wait a minute. How did Mahpiya know where Chrys was if she couldn't speak thought-to-thought with her yet?

Adonei told me, Mahpiya replied in a sultry purr. *He has been keeping me…company.*

'Oh, yeah? What kind of company, Mah?'

Do not play games with me, cub. You are aware we are mates. And while you have yet to secure your female, Adonei has wasted no time securing his.

Oh, god, he didn't want to know any more. Just the thought of mating was a seriously nasty turn-on. What the hell was wrong with him?

I always believed you were more lion than human, Mahpiya crooned. The transparent image of the majestic beast slowly groomed its paws.

Geri's voice streamed through the earpiece of the phone and broke through the private conversation between Rahn and his spirit guide.

"Rahn, are you there?"

"Uh, yeah, sorry, boss. Just thinking up various ways to keep Chrys off this case and out of danger without tying her up," he said, pacing again. But tying her up held a certain appeal. At least he'd know where she was.

"I don't envy you, Rahn. If she finds out you're spying on her, she may just kick your ass," she said glibly.

"I'm not really spying on her, just trying to keep her ass out of trouble. And if I recall, you sent me on this assignment, so my being here is your fault. I'll let her kick *your* ass," he chuckled. "I'll check in with you before I leave the ship at the next port."

"No problem. Talk to you later."

The second he clicked off the satellite phone and strode into the kitchen to hang it up, he called for his spirit guide again.

'Okay, now where is she?'

Did we not promise to help you, shall we say, ambush

*Chrysalyn? And so we shall.**

With that, the air in front of the pantry shimmered and shifted until it solidified into Mahpiya's corporeal body. She was such a powerful creature, so regal and perfect that Rahn almost regretted that no one could see or hear her except for him. He'd love to get a photo of her rolling from her side onto her back with her tongue lolling out. He'd never seen her so playful. That Adonei must be one hell of a man, er, lion.

*Do not concern yourself with my mate. We must help you win yours.** Then Mah stood with all the grace and attitude of the feline she was. She padded silently away. Rahn watched with curiosity. Where was she going?

The second the thought formed along the bond, the lioness swung her large head and pinned him with an amber stare.

Are you not coming, hoksila? *Your mate has gone to dinner. Surely you do not plan to go after her dressed like that.Besides, after your day of scouting, you smell…interesting.**

Then she laughed at him. Again. How the hell did she do that? And all at his expense. Good thing he knew she had his best interests at heart.

Less than half an hour later, Rahn and Mahpiya left the apartment. Rahn had to admit, it was pretty cool to walk down the wide civilized hallways with a bad-assed African lioness at his side.

Now all he had to do was capture a flesh and blood female hunter—Chrys.

* * * * *

Unlike this morning's breakfast bistro, this restaurant was dimly lit with an intimate atmosphere. The place was decked out for a performance of some kind of mystery song-and-dance dinner theater. A carpet of artificial fog crept across the floor, disturbed by the incoming crowd. Slightly scented votive candles glowed in the center of each table. The mystery in the air complemented the props and background music. Not creepy, but seductive.

Regardless of the lighting, two steps through the door, he spotted Chrys across the room and stopped short. She sat at a table with Eden Pall. Again. What the hell was she doing with that guy?

'Mah, you're aware of how I'm feeling?'

Aren't I always, hoksila?*

Yes, it was a stupid question, but he was pissed the hell off and couldn't say he was thinking rationally. But he was a master of pretending to be coolheaded.

'Be a dear and give Adonei a glimpse of my fabulous attitude so he can pass it on to Chrys, hm?'

I will do as you ask, my charge, though you may want to reconsider.

'Because?' he asked impatiently.

Because there are times when it is better to be wise rather than right.

'Perhaps. But not tonight. And while you're conversing with Adonei, lend me your senses. All of them.'

The raw power of the lioness surged through him, amplifying his own ability to see, hear, feel, taste and smell.

Rahn immediately regretted his request. Several women mingled in the small crowd between his position and Chrys' seat across the room. Their strong, much-too-flowery perfume stung his nose. Gah, how awful. He practically gagged.

Yet the strongest of the lioness's talents was sight. From this distance, he saw the nap of the viscose used to weave the cloth of Chrys' dress. The glittery lotion on her skin made the cinnamon shade appear dusted with diamonds. The candlelight reflected off the strands of cropped waves and curls on her lovely head.

He didn't miss the sudden rise of Chrys' chest. The quiet gasp told him the exact second Mah and Adonei passed his emotions on to her. She was getting more from him at this moment than either of them had bargained for. More anger than he'd ever expressed in word or deed. More raging possessiveness. More raw, erotic need.

Her big brown eyes found and then followed him as he wove his way around the tables. The place was packed with patrons who had no idea that a volatile situation had just walked in on two legs. Chrys' expression was a mix of confusion and apprehension and he knew she hadn't realized until now just how much he saw her as his. And she'd have an even clearer picture before the night was through. That was for damned sure.

The Eden creep spotted him as he made a beeline for their table. Why the hell did they have to pick one all the way on the other side of the room? Well, at least it was close to an exit door. Wait a minute. The Eden creep probably intended to whisk Chrys through that fucking door for a little evening interlude under the stars.

"Hello, love," Rahn whispered. A quick kiss on Chrys' cheek was followed by a steel-laced, "Eden, how nice to see you again."

Both occupants were doing a hell of a job schooling their features. Chrys' mouth hadn't fallen open nor had her eyes widened to the size of tea saucers. And Eden's distinct deep golden features were a blank mask. But this time, when the older man started to rise, Rahn moved smoothly with a gesture of conciliation.

"Please don't get up on my account. I'm not staying." *And neither are you*, he thought, taking in the display of Chrys' luscious curves, courtesy of a dazzling deep purple spaghetti strap dress. "Chrys, would you step outside with me for a moment. I called into the office today and I have a message for you." Well, it was true, just not in that order.

Ah, what a dazzling smile, Rahn grunted. He didn't appreciate she was giving it to the wrong man as she rose gracefully from the table, telling Eden she'd be right back. Rahn motioned toward the exit door not five paces from her chair.

The second she was over the threshold, he grasped her by the forearm, pulled her into the nearest alcove and completely lost his mind.

Chrys rounded on him, and hissed, "I was just about to have dinner, Rahn. This had better be important, damn it. So, what's the message?"

Angry didn't begin to describe her current mood, but he sensed she was more upset about her deepened breathing and the inability to suppress the flush of her skin. He inhaled deeply and was rewarded with the scent of her arousal. Mmm, the unique fragrance of her sex was just beginning to waft up from between her thighs. He grinned. The smell hadn't been there while she sat at the table, so at least she wasn't creaming for the Eden creep.

She'd asked him a question, but there was no way he could respond. Not now. Not when her sweet pussy called his name with its honeyed aroma. Not when his fingers itched to slide over her bare arms, the skin so smooth and soft, like endless candied silk stretched over sleek muscle. He almost cried out for God to help him when the tips of her nipples beaded and plumped under his gaze. His eyes followed the movement of her strong, slender fingers as they knotted into a fist and settled over her hip. And such a lovely hip—lush, full, wide and connected to a succulent, spankable ass that he wanted to grip, and then guide to his quickly rising erection.

"Rahn?" she asked grumpily. Now her left foot tapped on the floor of the alcove. Her perfectly polished nails peeked out of the tip of her strappy sandals. Painted to match the royal purple of her evening dress. Damn, even her feet were pretty. Each little digit looked just ripe for sucking. The image of his lips wrapped around each one made him look away and out toward the deck. The lacquered wood was awash in bright starlight, while the deep waters of the ocean reflected the bright moon like an endless sapphire pool. Definitely a night for lovers.

He remained silent. Her toe tapped faster.

"Rahn, I asked you a question."

Aw, hell.

"What's the message from Geri…mmmphff!"

It was moments like this when he was grateful he'd only asked Mahpiya to lend him her senses. If he'd asked for her supernatural strength, the rough way he'd grabbed Chrys might have bruised her tender skin. But damn, he needed to touch and he needed to touch her *now*. Smashed against his chest, her nipples tightened into teasing little treats hidden by the top of her dress. The sensual stab of the swollen points rasped against his skin through his linen shirt. Teased and tormented him because of his enhanced senses. His hands traveled the length of her back, following the curve of her spine as he dipped his head and took her mouth in a kiss so hot it singed the tips of his ears.

Her flavor burst upon his tongue. She tasted so good. Felt so good. As her apprehension melted away, her lips softened underneath his. Strong fingers sank into the front of his shirt and held on as she gave herself up to the kiss and let him feast as his tongue twisted and twined around hers.

He groaned into her mouth. His hand wandered up over her ribs and confirmed a niggling suspicion—she wasn't wearing a bra. The firm breast filling his palm was all her. God, such a curvy little thing. Perfect, pleasingly plump. And his.

Rahn left a trail of heated nips over the shell of her ear and down the slope of her neck. Her breathing deepened and he reveled in every rise and fall of her chest, the slight flush under her skin, the fullness of her kiss-swollen cherry lips.

One hand slid down over her hip and around to the plump globes of her ass. And he did exactly what he'd been thinking moments before. He pulled her hard against his groin and ground his hips forward. She looked surprised, thunderstruck and just a bit wary of her reaction to him. The woman seemed unsure whether to kiss him again or run like hell. His mouth kicked up into an irrepressible grin. He wanted to preen like Mahpiya did after a successful hunt. Why? The unflappable Chrysalyn Geyer was completely out of sorts and it was all his fault.

"Uh, so…my goodness," she said on a rush of breath. It took her a second to get it together. Then she let her artificial career agent's face slide into place.

She took a half-step back and said, "So, what's the message from work?"

She was too quick to recover. He'd have to work on that.

A rough edge he'd never experienced before with a woman rode him hard. The need to mark her, mate her was like a vise wrapped around his lungs that he'd never be free of until the deed was done. He'd never felt so predatory, so dangerous. Ever.

"First, I said I called in today. However, I did not say the message was from work."

"What?"

"Our boss says hi and enjoy your vacation. But the message, Chrys, is from me."

"Rahn, I don't understand. What message?" she said curtly, brows knitted with irritation. He knew what that meant. She wanted to know what was up. Right damned now. And Rahn wanted nothing more than to oblige.

"The message, love, is this—lose the Eden guy and meet me in our apartment in ten minutes. Or else."

"Or else? Really?" she said as the fist slammed back onto her hip. She couldn't tap her foot because he stood too close. "And what's the or else, asshole?"

One strong arm under her bottom lifted her clean off the floor, the other held her firmly, but gently, by the nape as he covered her mouth once again. Her legs automatically wrapped around his waist, causing her dress to ride up in a bunch around her hips. A single step had her back flush against the alcove wall as he kissed her hard, hungry. Miles and miles of gorgeous thigh and ass were bare to his questing fingers. And the scrap of cloth she called underwear was no barrier at all. A fingertip skimmed her left butt cheek. The nerves underneath her skin quivered clear down to the slit of her pussy. So he followed that quiver with his hands and allowed himself to play. Mmm, what a wonderland her body was.

Burning with need for this woman, Rahn poured the energy from the fire in his blood into the kiss, into each touch. God, he was going up in smoke. The ragged moans rising up in her throat told him she wasn't immune.

He eased away a bit and let her down. Her feet touched the ground and she wobbled. Well, maybe she didn't quite wobble, but it was an excuse to keep his hands on her a while longer. Unable to keep the rasp from his voice, he spoke through gritted teeth.

"Ten minutes, Chrys. Don't make me come looking for you."

Chest heaving, he backed away and disappeared out onto the deck. He didn't wait for a yes or no, didn't plan to give her a choice. And by the time he was done with her, she would only want to make one decision. Him.

The man was too damned bossy, but he sure had a talented tongue. Never mind the fact her heart had belonged to him for too many years to count. Even after he'd broken it, the bastard. She'd forgiven long before he'd ever apologized, so why did her heart and her head have such a hard time agreeing? One said he was the one for her. Even her spirit guide approved of the man. But the other said no way, that he would just hurt her again. She really needed some help here. She looked down at her watch. Seven minutes left to make up her mind.

'Adonei, come to me.'

Immediately, the semi-transparent image of her spirit guide's regal form appeared behind her eyes as she made her way back to the table where Eden waited. Other than Rahn, Chrys didn't think she'd ever met a more handsome man. And from Egypt, of all places, his home was just outside Alexandria, one of the ports of call on this trip. Maybe he would give her a personal tour of the Lighthouse of Pharos once they reached port?

A muted snuffle sounded in her mind as Adonei shook his maned head. *Your mate would not approve, woman.*

'But I haven't accepted him as my mate. I'm not sure I even want to.' Now why the hell had she bothered to say those words? Even if she tried to lie to herself, lying to Adonei was just plain impossible.

I cannot assist you if you are not willing to be honest.

'Yes, I know, Adonei,' she admitted with a sigh. She'd known the second Rahn laid down his little ultimatum what she would do. Would he always get his way? Hell no. After all, she was no punk bitch. But tonight, the man looked like a hunter after her hide, and she wanted to give it to him. She'd never felt such an innate need to submit before. Even when she'd been engaged to Sean, she would have laughed in his face if he'd ordered her to be somewhere. The difference was she wanted to be exactly where Rahn asked—no, told—her to be. In five more minutes.

"Hi, Eden. Sorry about the interruption," she said with the brightest smile she could muster. She didn't bother to sit down.

"Is something wrong, Chrysalyn?" he asked pointedly, but politely.

Honestly, she replied, "No, nothing's wrong." Adonei's rumble of approval resonated down their bond. "But I have to go. My coworker called into the office today." Which was true. "Something's come up." Yeah, Rahn's king of the jungle act, along with his thick cock. "I'm sorry, but I won't be able to stay for the dinner show. Maybe another time?"

There will be no other time, woman, Adonei shot down the bond. But she couldn't take the words back now and would just have to deal with it later.

Eden stood, graciously took her hand and kissed it

gently. "Another time, then. Do you require an escort?" he asked sweetly.

Adonei growled.

"No, thanks. I'll be fine. Goodnight, Eden."

She was sure he responded in kind, but she'd already made for the door.

Their condo was close now. If she hurried, she'd make it at exactly ten minutes. But running for any man was out of the question. Oh, she'd be there all right, honest enough with herself to admit she couldn't resist Rahn's call to her body, and had no desire to. But that didn't mean she couldn't take her time. Besides, she wore a formfitting dress and high heels, right?

Woman, if you were dressed in fitness wear and tennis shoes, you would still manage to be late, if only to prove a point.

'Adonei!'

But that was as far as her outrage carried, since the big cat was right.

CHAPTER SEVEN

The woman would choose now to be stubborn. Her ten minutes had come and gone. Rahn wished he could say the same for his Rock of Gibraltar erection. Walking over to the front door for the fifth time in as many minutes, he kicked his shoes off and paced back across the apartment.

Hands on hips, he stared out the sliding glass doors and past the private deck to the dark rolling ocean. He fisted his fingers in the thick drapes just to give his hands something to do. He wanted to play in her soft hair. Wanted to cup her firm ass and lift her against his throbbing cock. Fuck, he was going absolutely nuts.

Damned woman.

'Mah, where the hell is she?' Rahn growled silently.

I do not know, hoksila. There has yet to be an established bond between you and Chrysalyn, so I cannot yet touch her mind.

'Well, what about Adonei?' he snapped. 'Can't you just ask him?' He tore his hands away from the curtains, only to run them roughly through his own hair. The insistent need gnawing at his belly for this woman bordered on insane. If it was this bad now, how would it be after they established a relationship? She was five minutes late and he was practically out of his mind. Not something he was familiar with where a female was concerned. With the exception of Mahpiya's occasional absence from his head, Rahn had never been so impatiently alone.

He almost thrust his fingers down to his scalp again, but stopped himself, knowing what Chrys would see when she arrived—a wild-haired, crazed crackpot from the worst B movie he could imagine.

'Damn it, this is ridiculous, Mah. Why do I feel so out of control?'

It is the mating instinct. The need to claim your mate. Trust me, this is natural.

'How the hell would you know what's natural? First off, I'm a human, and second, I'm a male.'

Yes, which only makes you more irrational, cub. I suggest you calm yourself before your mate arrives.

Cub? Had she called him a cub? Rahn rolled his eyes. The lioness would choose this moment to remind him that he was no more than a child in her eyes. Her endless years and, of course, endless knowledge of dealing with humans gave her just a bit more of an edge in this situation.

He took a deep breath, closed his eyes and reached out for his guide, silently calling her onto this plane. Her big muscular body materialized, stretched out on the living room floor between the glass coffee table and the overstuffed couch. Rahn walked over and sat down on the floor next to her.

"I'm sorry, Mah," he said softly, reaching out a hand to rub her thick muscled shoulder. "I didn't mean to disrespect you. Forgive me?"

Of course, hoksila. As I said, you are less than rational. It is the mating heat and will ease once you claim your female. She is quite the prize. A strong hunter, though Adonei does not approve of her choice of casual companions.

"Her choice of what?"

But there was no answer. Without warning, Mahpiya's pelt shimmered and shifted. Her body faded until nothing but a faint dusting of her essence floated on the still air before disappearing all together.

"Mah?" All was quiet. Even the small, constantly occupied place in the corner of his mind was silent. It had only happened once before—this morning in the hot tub. He knew exactly what Mahpiya's sudden absence meant.

His cock twitched in anticipation as he sat there cross-legged on the floor, waiting for Chrys to turn the knob on the front door to their apartment.

* * * * *

Why did she feel like she was sneaking into her own place? Couldn't possibly have anything to do with the fact she was practically tiptoeing into her own foyer with her shoes in one hand and easing open the door with the other.

Rahn sat on the floor in the dark with a strange light in his eyes. Drapes pulled back, the wide glass panes allowed the evening light to flood into the room. The angle with which the beams reflected off his light amber orbs made him look like a cat caught by a flash of light.

He rose slowly, all sinewy grace and barely leashed power. Damned sexy.

Even the movement of his long legs and wide muscular torso reminded her of one of the big cats out hunting on the Serengeti. So entranced was she by the easy sway of his lean hips, the slight flex of biceps and pecs as he moved, Chrys didn't realize he was practically on top of her until they were toe to toe.

Then he had to go and open his fat mouth and ruin the moment.

"You're late. Where the hell have you been? And why didn't you check in with me earlier like I asked you to?"

Well, somebody wasn't happy, she mused sarcastically. At that exact moment, Adonei's presence diminished in her mind until he was barely a speck on the radar. Obviously backing off to leave her to deal with the miffed male towering over her.

'Traitor,' she hissed along the link. Good thing she

didn't expect a response because she received none.

"Chrys, I asked you a question, woman."

She snapped her neck to the side, knowing her eyes were wide with incredulity. Talk about a pissy attitude, the man was almost unbearable. The way he snarled down at her, she half expected him to start thumping his chest before tossing her over his shoulder while doing the Tarzan yodel.

Was this Rahn? The same Rahn she'd worked with for years? Cool, level-headed agent, laid-back, easy-going? Puh. Obviously not.

"You didn't ask me a question, Rahn, you asked me two," she snapped back, refusing to be treated like a damned child. Then again, she didn't recognize such behavior from this man, so she wasn't sure what he saw her as. Well, sizzling kisses and hot tub action aside, of course.

"Yeah, and you haven't answered either one of them."

The urge to submit to him while he'd held her up by her backside in a dark alcove just a little while ago faded as completely as Adonei had from her head. Challenge was the new word of the day.

"You're the one working here, Rahn. I'm on vacation. I'm playing."

"If you play with anyone, it sure as hell better be me!"

"What?" She couldn't believe what she was hearing. "Who the hell do you think you are? I am not accountable to you and owe you no explanations. I'll do what the hell I want, when I want. You're not my man, Rahn. Not anymore, if you ever were in the first place."

She was as hot as a Hawaiian volcano, and not with lust. Anger kindled so fast and high she expected his eyebrows to singe away any second now.

She dropped her shoes on the tiles next to his in the foyer, stepped around him with a humph and headed for her bedroom.

Who the hell did he think he was, anyway? She didn't

have to take this macho crap from anyone, damn it. *Even if you need a strong man to handle your stubborn female self?* She couldn't even scold Adonei for the comment because he hadn't made it. Damned conscience. It would choose this moment to show up.

Rahn was so close on her heels she'd swear she felt him breathing rough and hard down the back of her neck. Her arm froze in mid-reach for her doorknob when a firm, but gentle, hand teased her shoulder.

"Make no mistake about it, Chrys. I am your man."

The words were softly spoken, seductive with a hint of a growl. The deep rough timbre sent a thrill through her body. The enticing thrum began at her ankles, eased up the back of her calves and drilled into her thighs just below her butt. The flesh covering the sensitive spot between her ass and her pussy tingled and itched in anticipation of what would follow such a fierce declaration. A declaration he'd never made to her in all the long years they'd known each other.

She found herself spun around and eased back against her bedroom door. Mouths joined in a burning conflagration of lust, but she needed more than her lips on fire. She needed to completely go up in flames.

Chrys reached up to twine her arms around Rahn's neck, pressed closer and relished his shiver when iron-hard pecs made contact with puckering nipples. His chest muscles jumped and flinched. The involuntary movement made her peaks harden faster, stiffer.

Her own soft moans sounded eager and oh-so erotic in her own ears.

Rahn's arms tightened, totally engulfing her with his big beautiful body.

"Mmm, Chrys, baby," he moaned into her mouth, deepening the kiss, tasting, savoring. Overwhelming. "God, you taste so good."

Chrys broke away and rested her forehead against his chest, trying to get her catapulting emotions, not to mention her breathing, under control. But that didn't stop him from exploring her body with a knowledge that should be forbidden to any man on earth. It was just too devastatingly delicious.

He lowered his head and licked her overheated skin from her jawbone down to her collarbone. It felt so good, she could think of nothing to compare it to. When his hands cupped her ass, she didn't protest. As he teased and nibbled along her ear, her dress was hiked up past her hips to settle in silken rolls around her waist. Rahn's strong fingers continued to knead the flesh of her sensitive round cheeks. She gasped when a single finger eased into the cleft of her ass, then lower to the slick folds of her cunt.

It dipped and played until it was completely coated with the juices making their way down the inside of her thighs. Her hips made a perfect figure eight as she sought more of the intense pleasure.

When he removed his hand, Chrys caught the scent of her own dewy arousal. Damn, what a turn-on.

Rahn ground his thick erection against her hip as two fingers slipped up into her juicy pussy. With a subtle curve, the tips hit an overly sensitive bundle of nerves deep inside she hadn't known was there. He stroked once. Twice. Three times.

"Oh my god!" she screeched as that special little spot sent a crackling zing exploding through her womb. Every cell in her body screamed. Thigh muscles quivered while her ass clenched wildly and her fingers dug into Rahn's chest through his shirt. Head thrown back, it hit the door with a thump as she came on the spot.

Rahn dropped to his knees, buried his head between her legs and lapped up the fragrant evidence of her release. All the while, he hummed his approval as he wrapped his tongue around her throbbing clit, gently easing it out of its cowl and into his eager mouth. The combined vibration and suction shot up her slit and kicked off a new round of quivers stronger than the first. The earth shattered around her until she expected the ground to open up and swallow her whole.

"Rahn, please. I need you inside me."

He didn't stop moving his mouth over her flesh. Didn't stop humming over her clit. Didn't stop tormenting her with the long laps of his tongue or the fingers buried inside her.

Oh, and it was good. But damn it, she needed to be fucked. Hard, deep and long.

Reaching down, she sank her fingers into his hair, clear to the scalp and pulled. Easing him away from her soaked flesh, Chrys looked down and her eyes went wide. The man's mouth, nose and cheeks were covered with her own essence. His light brown eyes flashed with hunger and the hard set of his mouth told her she'd interrupted something he relished. And she'd better quickly replace it with something else.

He flashed a wicked grin while he massaged the backs of her knees. "You have interrupted my meal, Chrys."

Her mouth opened and snapped shut on a silent plea. God, he was so damned sexy she couldn't even form the words to describe his tousle-headed, handsome self. She tried to speak again just as his touch moved from the back of her right knee up to the juncture of her thighs and pressed into her swollen lips. Her breath hitched instead. Finally able to string more than two words together, they tumbled out as a strangled plea.

"Oh, Rahn, I need it. Please. Give it to me."

She needed this. Wanted this. Wanted him more than…hell, she couldn't think of anything or anyone that had ever made her feel so desperate. Not even the thrill of hunting and bringing down bad guys.

He grabbed a handful of dress and yanked. The sound of rending threads and popping straps resounded through the huge living room. The little scrap of soaked cloth partially covering her sex went next. Then she was underneath him on the floor.

Only one small problem. He still wore all his clothes.

Chrys sat up and pushed Rahn back on his knees. In a flash she'd unzipped his pants and pushed them down as far as they would go. Instead of taking his dark green silk boxers down with them, she bared his skin a scant bit at a time, nipping as she went. Her tongue flicked out and licked a spot just below his pelvic bone. He jerked, almost doubling over. So she tongued him there until he moaned nonstop.

"Chrys, god, baby! That feels so good."

But it wasn't nearly enough.

Finally her goal, his glorious hard cock, was completely uncovered. It bobbed in front of her face, the shaft a deep mottled caramel. The flared mushroom head wept. She could almost see the fat veins twined around it throbbing in time with her own rapidly beating heart.

The moment her fingers grasped the thick rod, a primal urge rippled through her soul. The need to mark herself with his scent. To be his, and for him to be hers. Leaning forward, Chrys gently rubbed the smooth hard length of him against her cheek. Then across her forehead and down the other side of her face before turning to take him down her throat in one gulp. His scent filled her nostrils even as he filled her mouth.

He yelled. Thighs shook, hands clenched wildly at his sides. The taut tendons of his throat stood out from his neck as he hissed through gritted teeth.

"Aaaah, shit! Chrys!" he pleaded, took in a large gulp of air and begged some more. Just as she'd begged moments before. "Woman, you're killing me."

Humming around his cock certainly wouldn't make it any easier on him, but she felt particularly evil just now and planned to drive him as insane as humanly possible.

He must have caught on when she didn't stop sliding her tongue over him, didn't stop stroking him. She knew the jig was up when he eased her away from his cock. Pants were kicked off, shirt yanked over his head and hands reached out for her. In a split second, she was settled with her creaming slit directly over his hungry cock.

And just when she thought he would plunge to the hilt, he scooped her up in one hand and flipped them both until he was dominant.

Her pussy was so swollen, it throbbed to the point of pain. If he didn't fuck her soon, she would lose it. Her lower lips were so puffy and wet, dew dribbled and pooled into the crack of her ass, making her cheeks clench spasmodically.

Finally he pressed into her sopping entrance.

Only the head of his cock dipped into her scalding pussy, yet it almost did him in. Rahn couldn't believe how close he was to totally losing control and coming right then and there. Gritting his teeth, he reined in the wild urge to surge to the hilt and camp out there for the rest of the night.

Then she moved.

Shit. So much warm slick flesh slid against his, while her cunt pulled on him, begged for the very thing he was trying to hold back. Lowering his head, Rahn sought her lips and poured all his desire and every downright nasty inclination into that lip lock. Her tongue boldly tasted his, joined in a magical dance that sent his head spinning as he slowly eased deeper into her body.

The walls of her sweet channel closed in around his length and squeezed. The woman was absolutely delicious. So wet, tight and his.

The exquisite friction of sliding his hardness into her hot, sopping flesh sent a tremor clear down to the fine hairs on his toes. Rahn couldn't let another second tick by without having them joined lip to lip, chest to chest and cock to pussy.

The inside of Chrys' strong thighs rubbed against his hips as she wrapped her legs around him. Settling her heels into the base of his spine, she tightened her grip and urged him deeper. God, the woman squeezed him everywhere—

cock, waist, spine. Not to mention the arms wrapped firmly around his back, holding him so tight, he struggled to breathe. Then again, the demanding rhythm of Chrys' hips keeping time with every thrust of his rod may have had something to do with the lack of air in his lungs. She sucked the very life out of him. And damn, he liked it.

"God, love, you feel so good wrapped around my cock." Rahn eased out slowly, his throbbing erection coated with her dewy juices. "Come for me, Chrys." A ruthless, balls-deep plunge back into her depths. "Come around my cock. Milk me, love."

Her eyes were glazed over with passion. Her answering pant and moan preceded a gentle nudge against his shoulders. Reluctantly, he eased his weight off her and pushed up on his palms. Rahn sucked in a shallow breath at the rush of air flowing between them, cooling the heated flesh of his pecs. That single breath remained locked in his airway after Chrys' hand disappeared into the space between their bodies.

His stomach muscles clenched wildly as her fingers traipsed over the ridges. But she didn't stop there. The woman teased past his abs and wrapped her fingers around the base of his cock just as he pushed forward into her pussy again.

"If I go, you go...oh, oh," she squealed.

The inviting "O" of her luscious lips made him wish he had two cocks, one for her mouth and one for her pussy. Eyes closed, he knew the moment her fingers reached her clit. The quiver and pulse of her sex was immediate.

Death was imminent. There was no way he'd survive such exquisite pleasure. The sensation of her cunt encircling him, combined with the fingers traveling from her clit back to the base of his cock over and over again, shredded any bit of imagined control.

"Oh god, fuck me!" she demanded.

He drove into her, then pulled back until just the flared head remained inside. Then buried himself again. Fast.

Faster.

She panted and moaned, mixing an occasional "Oh my god!" with Rahn's own wild grunting.

Just before he went up in flames, Rahn lowered his head and sank his teeth into the soft flesh between Chrys' shoulder and neck. Not enough to draw blood, but enough to still the wild thrashing and clawing as she sought her own release.

With a final thrust of his hips, he slammed into her cervix with a mix of pleasure and pain. Sleek pussy walls pulsed around his erupting cock and they came together with an intensity that yanked a roar of completion from his throat and a sensual scream from Chrys.

His arms gave out and he collapsed on top of her. He sighed while her fingers lazily traced the bones of his spine through the light sheen of sweat cooling on his skin. Sliding toward what he knew would be the sweetest sleep he'd had in a while, he was taken by surprise when Chrys flipped them over, her sweet cunt still clasped around his softening cock.

Mimicking his behavior of only moments before, she bit into his thick trapezius muscle between neck and shoulder. The sting of the bite sent a blazing rush of blood to reawaken his cock. He'd never recovered this quickly before, yet here he was instantly hard and just as hungry for the woman as the first time.

Thank god Chrys was already impaled on his flesh. There was nothing to delay him pumping like a madman while she kept a grip on his neck.

She bit down harder. He bucked like an unbroken bronco and she rode him like the most experienced cowgirl until they once again fell apart in each other's arms.

CHAPTER EIGHT

Rahn rolled over with a groan. The goofy grin on his face disappeared when his hand made contact with a cold pillow where Chrys' head should have been.

"Damned woman. Why can't she stay where I put her?"

Mahpiya yawned big in his head. *It will take more than a bite on the neck to tame that one. Then again, perhaps you do not wish to tame her at all.*

Hmm. Well, maybe not. After all, the whiny doormat type had never appealed to Rahn. Chrys was his equal in every way. She was a hell of an undercover agent, educated, honorable, loyal. She didn't take any crap off anyone for any reason, but also knew when to negotiate. And she'd try her best to kick his ass if he ever pissed her off enough and then was stupid enough to let his guard down. Yes, she was a challenge. A worthy mate.

Their mating was far from complete, but last night had certainly been a fabulous start. Now all he had to do was get her to accept him completely, to accept what they were to each other. And he was certainly up to the task.

He ducked back into his bedroom for a quick shower. Dressed in nothing but a pair of comfortable jeans, Rahn grabbed his secure satellite phone off the nightstand and spoke into the voice recognizer.

"Dial Mother Hubbard."

After a few *clicks*, ringing sounded through the earpiece.

"Stud, here."

"Hey, Geri. Just checking in."

"How's the investigation going?"

"The captain has provided me with more good information. And since I can't get him to stay out of this, we've come up with a plausible excuse for him to accompany me here and yon. He's going to play tour guide."

"And how's Chrys?"

"A handful if ever she was, Geri."

"Has she figured out anything since the last time we talked?"

"Hell, no. But if I know Chrys, she's just not saying anything."

"You've got that right, Rahn. Just be careful. If you get hurt on this mission, Chrys will have your head. If she hasn't, er, had it already."

"A gentleman wouldn't dare go there. But I will say that I certainly have a better reason to be on this ship than finding a serial killer."

"Is that reason about five-foot-nothing with a muscular build, short wavy hair and brown eyes?"

"Actually, yes. I'll call you when I have something more to report, all right, boss?"

"Right. Mother Hubbard, out."

He snapped the phone closed and stuffed it in the back pocket of his jeans. Barefooted, he padded to the kitchen, pulled some fresh greens from the fridge and sat them on the built-in chopping board on the counter.

Suddenly, he wasn't in the mood to cook. In fact, he didn't want to eat either, not unless Chrys was on the menu.

Leaning against the nearest wall, Rahn reached out

along the bond with his spirit guide.

'Mah?'

Her ears perked forward. *Yes, hoksila?*

'Where is my mate?'

Shouldn't you know? she teased.

But, yeah, he should know. And if he had anything to say about it, he would know from now on.

'Mah, would you mind…'

Yes, I know, my dear. Would I mind asking my Adonei where she is?

He felt like a little kid again, but smashed down his pride and muttered, 'Uh, yes, ma'am.'

After a moment of silence, Mah's thoughts filled his head along with the images she'd borrowed from Adonei. Chrys was in the exact spot he'd found her yesterday morning—in their private hot tub.

He picked up the phone and dialed the food service people.

"Hello, this is Rahn Benson in 15E. We require the service of the personal chef for breakfast, lunch and dinner. I have a menu in mind. If you can have a chef arrive within the hour, he can fix all the meals and we'll reheat them later. Oh, and I'll leave the front door unlocked. We'll be busy."

Rahn hung up the phone, strode to his room and dropped his jeans in the middle of the floor. The glass doors that led from his room to the balcony moved on silent tracks. He stepped out and there she was. Arms spread wide, head thrown back and resting on the edge of the tub, Chrys looked to be asleep. Then a forearm moved, bent at the elbow until a hand settled on her right breast and caressed with care. Her head rolled from one shoulder to the other. She sighed and dropped her hand back to the side of the tub.

Damn, she had such lovely breasts. Rahn could see the outline of her nipple straining against the fabric of her royal blue bikini from here. And the stiff little peak called his name, begged him to come set it loose so it could greet the morning sunshine.

Rahn padded to greet his mate.

* * * * *

My god, what was she going to do? How the hell was she supposed to make it through this whole vacation with both her heart and pussy intact with a virile man like Rahn sharing her apartment?

Did she want him? Absolutely. But what if it didn't work out again?

The man seemed to be all into her right now, but what if he changed his mind?

Chrys tilted her head back to rest against the ledge of the hot tub. She tried to relax and let the hot bubbling water melt away her troubles. A glass of her favorite juice sat at her fingertips. A wisp of smoke from her favorite Kahlua mini-cigar floated up and mingled with the steam of the hot tub. And she hadn't taken a single sip or puff. None of it appealed, given the butterflies dive-bombing her stomach.

Then she thought of how she'd tiptoed from her own bed in the early hours of the morning, and the butterflies were driven off by a band of ravaging ravens. She really needed help here.

'Adonei?'

I am here, Chrysalyn. Shall I come to you?

Her throat clogged with unexplainable tears. 'Yes, please.'

Adonei's powerful tawny body shimmered into view next to the hot tub just within arm's reach. Chrys stretched her arm toward him and sank her fingers into the thick dark mane. He turned questioning brown-sugar eyes on her, and suddenly she wanted to hide, to sink under the turbulent water until it was over her head.

Why are you so upset, Chrysalyn?

'Because I don't know what to say or how to act the next time I see Rahn. Sure, he did the you-my-woman thing last night. In fact, he did it quite well.' Her womb fluttered at the memory of what a fantastic lover Rahn had been. Every touch had brought her pleasure. No awkward moments. No missteps or blunders. It had been, in a word, perfect. 'But that doesn't mean he'll be as sure about this, this…whatever it is between us now that morning is here.'

Woman, you make no sense. You had no problem facing him after coming together in the warm pool before.

'Hot tub, Adonei,' she huffed.

As you wish. However, if you were able to face him then, you can face him now. He is your mate, you are meant to be. He knows this as well as you, yes?

'Yes, I know he's my mate.' A deep sigh followed the admission she didn't think she'd ever make, simply because she hadn't expected to have Rahn.

Then why would he not want you as much in the light of day as he did under the light of the moon?

'It's just that before, when we had a chance to be together, it didn't work out. And, well…hell, you know what happened. You were my spirit guide, after all.'

Yes, the spirit guide who tried to tell you…

'I know, Adonei, I know. You tried to tell me I was tripping and that he wasn't serious about the woman he was working that case with.'

Yet you still chose to become engaged with that dreadful what's-his-name.

Chrys grimaced. Sheesh, talk about the disaster of a lifetime. And she'd been so determined to walk into the disaster just to make Rahn jealous, it took her almost-mom-in-law disclosing the secret from hell to shake her resolve—she would have been wife number four. And it wasn't just the number of marriages that made her back up and take stock, it was the fact the asshole hadn't told her then, and still wouldn't own up to it. Not to mention the way he'd gotten rid of wife number one. The sneaky bastard had movers come while he was at work, pack the woman up and ship her off. When he got home that evening, he was happily wifeless.

Unfortunately, by the time Chrys had come to her senses and broken off the engagement, Rahn had moved back to London.

Now here she was with a second chance to be with the man of her dreams and fear had her damn near paralyzed…unless she was in his arms being fucked silly, of course. In truth, other than the constant state of horny-ness since Rahn showed up on her doorstep, Chrys was scared down to her toes.

Do not worry, woman. There are events in motion larger than yourself. And they are all good things. Trust your instincts and listen to your guide. Neither of us has ever led you astray, yes?

'Yes, you're right. Thanks, Adonei.'

Of course, I am right, he sniffed, all smug male lion.

His ever-present place in her mind lessened and the big cat's corporeal form glimmered and faded. Her stomach knotted nervously.

Chrys scented Rahn as he approached and almost groaned. She hadn't had time to completely process the meaning of the explosive bout of lovemaking—scratch that—no-holds-barred jungle fucking they'd done on the living room floor. There was no way she could handle a confrontation with him right now.

Adonei popped back in long enough to say, *And you know it will be a confrontation because…?*

'Oh hush, already,' she admonished.

Her eyes flew open on a squeak when she found herself hauled up against a hard chest, then set on her feet on top of the bath seat. Rahn nuzzled her navel as she stood in front of him.

"I don't like waking without you, Chrys."

Tilting her head to the side, she settled a fist on her hip. Was the man growling at her?

Ignoring her posturing, he continued. "It makes me think…"

She sucked in a breath when her bikini top flew across

the deck and the ocean breeze teased her nipples.

"That you regret our time spent together last night."

The man skipped all the preliminary niceties. Hell, he hadn't even kissed her. Just picked her up and dove for her pussy like his lifetime supply of breakfast, lunch and dinner oozed from her rapidly swelling sex.

He backed off long enough to ask, "Do you regret it, Chrys?"

"I-I, no. I don't, uh. Oh god."

How the hell was she supposed to think, talk and feel all at the same time, damn it?

His warm tongue slipped between her pout folds, wreaked havoc on her senses. Fingers eased up and down her bare thighs as his mouth devoured her on the spot.

With her bikini bottom scrunched off to the side, he soon grumbled his frustration at the fabric impeding such important progress. But he couldn't bear to let her move more than an inch from his questing mouth. She tasted so good. Felt so good. He knotted his fist in the stretchy fabric and yanked. The remnants of the bottoms joined the bikini top across the deck.

Her very loud "damn it" told him she wanted to fuss. Instead, it came out a moan as his fingers found a home deep inside her gripping heat. He looked up in time to watch her mouth fall open. Wide enough to slip a nice wide cock into. His breath caught in his throat and rumbled around in his chest as he fought to keep his feet planted on the floor of the hot tub rather than springing up and tackling her to the deck.

He'd always had finesse with his lovers, but Chrys sent his brain into overload. He had no class, no James Bond-type subtlety where she was concerned. It was all out there for her to see, laid bare and downright greedy for her. But he was a man of control. Puh. Right.

"Touch your beautiful breasts, baby. I love it when you touch yourself."

His gaze settled on the palms of her hands as she

caressed and weighed the caramel-tipped beauties. Mmm, and the way her fingers tweaked and rasped over the sweet nipples until they were stiff and distended had his eyeballs bulging along with his cock. And her soft moans and writhing hips? Aw fuck.

To hell with it. Grabbing her by the waist, Rahn carried her, with her delectable ass pressed against his cock, to the nearest balcony door. Setting her on her feet, he pressed her up against the sliding glass doors.

"Rahn, what the hell…?" she demanded. But that was as far as she got.

The man palmed the sides of her firm succulent breasts as he smashed her against the cool panes. A needy cock plowed into her from behind in one frantic stroke.

"Oh yes. Oh dear god, that's so good." The wicked swivel of her hips pulled him deeper. "Mmm, yeah. That's it, baby, fuck me."

He grinned at the smudged fingerprints on the glass where she clawed at the window with each deep stroke.

There it was again. Perfect, exhilarating friction and heat wrapped around his rod on each glide in, each slide out. He looked down to where their bodies came together. The sweet cunt gobbling up his cock provided the first course of a succulent erotic feast for the senses. Engaged in every way, he reveled in the sight, sound, taste, feel and scent of her pleasure. Thick honeyed dew became a froth of cream at her entrance. More. He had to have more.

"Give me that cream, love. Come for me, Chrys."

He gripped a thigh, lifted it high and was rewarded with a deep gasp as her sugared walls tightened and fluttered.

"Oh god. Sssss, Rahn. Oh yeeeesssss!"

Rahn scooped her up just as her knees buckled. Planted firmly in her still-twinging pussy, he eased open the glass doors and stepped into her bedroom.

They never made it to the bed…but the lovely floor-to-ceiling mirrors on her closet door provided some nice images he would remember until the day he died.

* * * * *

Mahpiya stretched out on her stomach, paws crossed lazily as she purred. Adonei laved the base of her neck with long swipes of his rough-textured tongue. An occasional nip of his sharp teeth produced a quivering in her stomach and a satisfied rumbling in her throat.

God, the lion sure could groom.

"So," she hummed. His tongue eased over a particularly sensitive spot just below her ear. "I do believe our charges are getting along rather nicely."

"Yes, I agree. My Chrysalyn can be rather stubborn at times, yet I believe she understands the significance of her attraction to your Rahn."

"I am glad they have finally reached the point in their lives where they can accept a mating. When they were together before, I did not sense you as I do now," Mahpiya whispered around a yawn.

"Perhaps the Great Spirit meant for us to help train our charges, ready them for a time such as this? It would not have been possible to keep me away from you if I had been aware of you back then. The results would have been less than helpful to either Chrysalyn or Rahn."

Mahpiya thought it over and decided her mate's words made sense. If she and Adonei had gotten together before Chrys and Rahn were ready to mate, one of them would have had to give up being a spirit guide.

It was uncommon enough for a female guide to be given to a male human. But the Great Spirit simply wouldn't have allowed Mahpiya to continue to guide and protect Rahn if she mated with Adonei, but Rahn didn't accept Chrys. So to avoid such an incident, it made sense that the Great Spirit had simply hidden Adonei and her from each other. Until now.

Sigh. And what a lovely now it was.

Thoughts of Rahn's case intruded on her contentment. Adonei immediately picked up on it and settled his big muscular body down next to hers, pressing his sides against her. The significance of the simple act reassured and infused her with warmth. He truly was a magnificent animal, her lion.

"Adonei, I am concerned about the killer my charge is tracking. It is a dangerous business. We have always worked well together on things such as this, yet I feel as if I am blinded from things I would typically be aware of."

"Yes, I understand. It is the same with me. And more concerning is that Chrysalyn knows your charge is here for more than a simple ride to Rome. Yet she says nothing because she is afraid."

"Afraid of what? The Eden fellow? He makes it no secret that he wants her."

"No, Chrys thinks nothing of him. My charge is not easily frightened, but her desire for her mate is almost overwhelmed by fear of losing Rahn now that they have found each other again. But speaking of the Eden fellow, he seems to appear whenever she is not with your charge. There is something about him that bothers me. I am sure he is a danger to Chrysalyn."

"Yet you have chosen not to tell her this. Why?"

"It is not my place. It is for your charge to discover the danger and keep her from it."

"Ah," she said. "Perhaps my Rahn's mission and the danger surrounding your Chrys are one and the same. If this is the case, I see why we would be prohibited from interfering too much. Looking after Chrys is something Rahn would wish to do with as little interference from me as possible. It is in his nature to want to protect his female."

"And I will protect mine," Adonei growled as he moved to cover her.

Mmm, there were times like this that Mahpiya more than appreciated being a spirit guide. Unlike natural lions, Mahpiya and Adonei could shift into a human representation of their lion selves, and couple for much longer than just a few moments And right now she reveled in the tantalizing sensation of her lover moving inside her, hard and fast, just the way she liked it. Strong teeth sank gently into her neck, keeping her immobile for his ravishing. Instinctive behavior for a male, but it was far from necessary. The loving felt so good, staying like this as he plunged into her hungry core was no certainly hardship.

CHAPTER NINE

The second the chef finished preparing their meals, Rahn shook the man's hand with a grin and practically shoved him out the front door. He was already on his way back to Chrys' bedroom when Mahpiya brought a message from Adonei. Chrys was still asleep. The male spirit guide would have usually roused her when the chef, a stranger, arrived. This time, he deliberately didn't wake her.

'Mah, ask him why he didn't warn Chrys that I was in the apartment the night I came aboard and Chrys almost whipped my ass in the dark?'

He says because he felt me, sensed my essence within you. He, he…scented me.

Well, this was a first. Mah was embarrassed. Another question for the list of things to ask God when he got to heaven—how the hell did a lioness blush?

Rahn chuckled. Mah growled.

'Oh, don't be offended. It's funny.'

Eyes closed, he grinned at the faint image of the majestic cat licking her paws with a disgruntled snap of her tongue. Her tail swished up into the air. He knew if she'd been on this plane, she'd have swatted him with it. She was such a doll.

On to more important matters, shall we? You have a concern, do you not, hoksila?*

'Actually, I do. I'm just not sure how to approach Chrys with the whole mating, bonding thing. I'd never expected to find a mate who had a spirit guide like me. A spirit guide I'm not supposed to know anything about.'

He shucked his robe and let it fall to the floor next to the bed as he joined his woman under the covers. Chrys' warm body instinctively snuggled up to his.

Your Chrysalyn may be skeptical at first, but Adonei and I are both here. She will believe you because she believes Adonei. Now is as good a time as any other to discuss such an important subject.

'I know you're right, Mah. I just wish I knew what Chrys was thinking.'

You are a wise man. You will choose your words carefully and all will work out in the end. Besides, your female is just as wise.

'Thanks for the encouragement, Mah. Stick around in case I need you, all right?'

Of course.

Mahpiya turned and padded away. Her image, but not her presence, faded from behind his eyes. At ease, yet ever watchful, the huge cat settled into her favorite spot.

Reassured, Rahn sent one last thought to her before he woke his mate.

'I love you, Mah.'

Yes, but not as much as you love her, which is as it should be.

Wow. Was Mahpiya right? He had strong feelings for Chrys, but was he already far gone in love with her?

It was a stupid question. He'd always loved her, even after they'd shattered each other's hearts.

He lay there for long moments, contemplating how to go about what he knew must be done. Chrys shifted in his arms. A satisfied sigh escaped her lips as the fragrance of their loving wafted from underneath the sheets. Their scents mingled and Rahn came to an immediate conclusion—he smelled damned good on her.

Easing his fingers along her jawbone, he gently tapped

her.

"Chrys, sweetheart, wake up."

"Mmmnnn, no wanna." She grumbled, turned over and scooted her lovely backside up against his thigh.

Instant erection. Damn.

Ignoring the throbbing cock now tenting the sheets, he hauled her up against his chest and whispered in her ear.

"Chrysalyn, do you believe in spirit guides?"

He almost laughed when her neck jerked back as if he'd smacked her. Honey brown eyes snapped open, along with her lush kiss-swollen lips. She quickly painted on a plastic smile and a bland expression, but too late.

Well, he certainly had her attention.

"Do I believe in what?" she asked, her tone one of incredulity mixed with a bit of agitation. And was that a hint of fear in her eyes?

Wrapping her in his arms, Rahn settled her more comfortably against his chest in a gesture he hoped was reassuring.

"Spirit guides, sweetheart." When she didn't respond, he sat up, taking her with him. Her warm, moist pussy settled right against his raging hard-on. Damn, it was difficult to hold a conversation when all he really wanted to do was melt into her.

Instead, he looked in her eyes and said, "Look, Chrys, I want to share all of myself with you. And that includes my spirit guide."

She still hadn't said a word.

'Okay, Mah. Help me out here…'

Adonei says Chrys is wondering how someone of your origins could have a spirit guide.

Duh. Made sense. Of course she would wonder. Spirit guides were a Native American thing. Chrys' Lakota Sioux grandma made sure she and her cousins grew up with a clear understanding and appreciation for both natural and spiritual things. He knew this because, even though he was a blue-blooded Englishman and half Egyptian, it was

Chrys' cousin's fault he'd met Mahpiya in the first place.

"Chrys, you're probably wondering how someone like me could have a spirit guide, right?"

"Uh, er, well…" she sputtered, pulling the sheets up to obstruct his view of her beautiful plump breasts.

"No worries, love. After all, spirit guides are a Native thing, while I'm white and Egyptian."

"But, Rahn, you don't have to…"

"Hush, sweetheart, I do indeed have to. Now listen, all right?"

Rahn was pleased when the woman snapped her mouth shut and listened as he recounted a case he'd worked as a young agent. Chrys' cousin, Delaine Jeris, had been assigned to mentor him, and took him along on one of her cases. One particular mission involved corruption, murder and, unfortunately, federal agents. To this day, neither Rahn nor Delaine had ever spoken a word of the happenings of that incident to anyone except their boss. Until now.

Thankfully, his heritage came with the luxury of a deep tan during the summer months and allowed Delaine and him to go deep undercover on a reservation in South Dakota. The same reservation both Delaine and Chrys had visited often during their growing-up years.

During his extended stay on the res, Delaine quietly took him to spend time with their grandma. She was a wise old woman, wise in the ways of spirit and life. She'd patiently shared her experiences with him between cups of strong coffee and piles of homemade fry bread sprinkled with powdered sugar or honey.

The Lakota believed that the Great Spirit, Wakantanka, created all things and was no respecter of persons. Granny often laughed when she said, "Wakantanka will not hold it against you that you were not born a Sioux."

Rahn had gained a new respect for the land and nature. Learned about spirit guides and himself, as well as the importance of understanding his place in the world. The time Delaine and Granny spent teaching him about Lakota beliefs and customs not only helped him understand and have patience with others, but it saved his life.

"While checking out a lead, I was snatched out of my car, bashed over the head and dragged out into the middle of nowhere." Chrys winced. With a chuckle full of mirth, he said, "It got better. I was then shot and left for dead almost fifty miles from the nearest warm body. I called out to the Great Spirit with all my heart, just like Granny, *your* Granny, taught me. In that moment, Mahpiya came to me."

Chrys' eyes gleamed with unshed tears as he described the calm that had enveloped his mind. A peace so encompassing, he knew he was going to die. Just when he thought he'd taken his last breath, Mahpiya spoke to him.

I have come to protect and guide you, hoksila. *I will be with you for as long as you wish. Do you accept me?*

At his mental nod, the image of the most majestic creature he'd ever seen, a huge and powerful African lioness, appeared behind his eyes. In that instant, the connection, the bond they shared to this very day, snapped into place.

Take what I offer, my charge.

The words preceded a ferocious surge of power that slammed into his physical body, giving him the strength to make it to the nearest road. Thankfully, a stranger stopped and took him to the hospital.

"Chrys, baby, are you crying?"

She shook her head, but a loud, slurpy sniff gave away how touched she was by his story.

"Chrys, you're my mate and I want you more than anyone or anything. But…" He paused and took a breath. "My spirit guide is important to me. Can you accept both of us? I understand there are old fears that make you want to pull away from me and not trust me. I'm sorry for that, but can you let it go? Especially since neither of us meant to hurt one another."

Her eyebrows rose a good inch.

"Yes, Chrys, you hurt me too. But I know you didn't mean to and I forgave you a long time ago."

Rahn sat quietly, stroking the short silky curls she sported so well. He swore he heard the gears turning in her head as she worked out her feelings. No problem. There was only one thing left to say.

"Chrys, I swear I'll be yours for as long as you'll have me, love. Take the time you need to think about it, but let me be clear. I don't intend to take no for an answer."

Chrys tried to stem the flow of tears, but simply couldn't. She knew what it took to share something as intimate as a spirit guide, how important it was to guard such a special connection with a creature not of this world. But Rhan shared his Mahpiya without hesitation. Knowing Rahn's spirit guide must have sensed Adonei by now, the tears ran faster down her cheeks—the man hadn't asked a single question about her own special circumstances.

The fortified walls around her heart crumbled. All the fear and pain she'd kept closed inside melted away. Chrysalyn wanted him more than ever. But...

'Adonei?'

Warmth trickled down their psychic bond.

Go ahead, Chrysalyn. Share yourself with your mate. The result will be a love you have never imagined.

It was all the encouragement she needed. She took in a shuttering breath and resisted the urge to wipe her face on the warm skin of Rahn's chiseled pecs.

"Rahn," she blubbered, so moved it didn't enter her mind to be embarrassed. "I don't need time to think about it, I know what I want. And that's you. And I have a spirit guide too. His name is Adonei, an African lion."

Rahn shifted enough to reach over to the nightstand and pass her a handful of tissues. Blowing rather unceremoniously, she cleaned her face, wiped away the tears...and her logical agent's brain jumped into the silence.

Wait a minute. How much of a coincidence was it that Rahn's spirit guide was an African lioness and hers was an African lion? Was she missing something here?

Suddenly, a pair of strong hands picked her up and placed her chest to chest, thighs spread, with a meaty erection pressed against her clit. Every curious thought trickled right out of her head when the man slid his hard cock back and forth across the little bundle of nerves, urging her body to release its slick, moist dew. Didn't take long.

Oh lord. What had she been thinking about? Wait, Rahn's lioness…

"Mate with me?" he asked softly. Leaning forward, a warm tongue wrapped around a plump nipple and tugged lightly. His hips moved slowly, sinuously, back and forth, rubbing, sliding, encouraging. "Chrys?"

"Oh god, yes," she sighed. Head thrown back, she rose up on her knees just enough to make clearance for his upright shaft. She laced her fingers behind her head and watched his skilled fingers move over her sensitive skin. One hand gently spread her swelling pussy lips while the other eased the tip of his cock inside.

Then came a faint stirring in her mind. Adonei? How strange. This time her guide hadn't left her as he had the other times she and Rahn had made love. This time, the second Rahn's hard length disappeared inside her hungry pussy, she felt a presence join Adonei.

Hello, wicincala. I am Mahpiya, come to aid our mates in your protection and guidance. I will be with you for as long as you wish. Do you accept me?

'You've come to aid our mates? I don't understand,' Chrys gasped as the head of her man's cock parted her flesh.

Mahpiya answered her question almost before it fully formed in her head.

Adonei is my mate. My charge, Rahn, is yours. I would join with both of you. And no, the males cannot hear us. This is a moment *for just the two of us.**

'What about later?'

All will be explained in due time. Now is the time for mating. Do you accept me?

'Yes. Yes, of course.'

Suddenly the flame of desire between her and Rahn erupted into a conflagration of care and flat-out lust. Strong enough, powerful enough to singe her very soul. It was the merging, the mating of their spirit guides combined with her and Rahn's joining.

Mahpiya's rumbled purr subsided and Rahn's rough-edged voice filled her ears.

"Ride me, Chrys. Ride my cock, love."

Hands cupped underneath her backside, he lifted her until he was nothing more than a tease at her entrance. Raising his hips, he slammed her body down to meet his and sank deep inside. Again. And again. Until she was a trembling mass of need.

"That's it, Chrys. Take it, take all of me."

Hell, she didn't think it was physically or spiritually possible to take anything more. Inside her head, she couldn't see Adonei and Mahpiya mating, but she sure as hell sensed it. The loving was fierce, untamed. Wild. The sensation of feral heat zinged back and forth along the psychic bond with Adonei, now made doubly strong by Mahpiya's presence.

It called to her and she opened herself to it completely, allowed it to surge through her blood. The need was so strong, she was filled with it. Brimming over until she expected the very cells underneath her skin to catch fire.

Her pussy tightened and clenched around her lover's thrusting cock. Oh god, it was so good. So hot. So deliciously wanton.

"Damn, woman! Oh, yeah, just like that," Chrys heard Rahn growl. His words only ratcheted up the heat as his molten length pistoned into her wet cunt with supernatural speed. And she received him with supernatural endurance.

Whoa. Their guides had given them their power without asking? Reassurance flooded her soul and she knew this was part of the mating heat between them and their lions.

And it was damned near too much. Chrys couldn't remember ever being this overwhelmed by a bout of sex in her life. It was out of this world. Literally.

"God, Rahn, you feel so good."

"Then come for me, sweetheart. Bathe my cock."

Her stomach muscles trembled and tightened in cadence with her pulsing sex. When his fingers left her breast and focused on her clit, she yelled to the rafters.

"I can't," she wailed. "It's too much. It just feels too good. I can't take it!"

"You can," Rahn asserted. "And you will." His voice was tight, rough. His fingers trembled and his chest rose and fell with deep, but erratic gusts. Well, at least she wasn't the only one losing her mind.

The friction between their bodies was exquisite. He slammed into her, out of her, so fast that her juices ran down the inside of her thighs like the froth on her morning cappuccino.

"Oh god. Oh, shit. Rahn!"

"That's it, baby. Give it to me. Give it to me, now."

They orgasmed as one. His cock pulsed and exploded deep inside her just as her channel squeezed and milked him. Their worlds collided, bright and cataclysmic, leaving the earth trembling in the wake.

As Chrys drifted toward sweet oblivion, her mind was bathed with a soothing blanket of love. Mahpiya's, Adonei's. And Rahn's.

* * * * *

Rahn rolled over and reached for his new mate. A satisfied sigh became a frustrated groan. Chrys was gone. Again.

"Damn it, what is it with that woman never being where she's supposed to be?" he grumbled to himself. After reviving from her faint—something she swore never happened, period—the woman wore his balls into the mattress with a fierce loving that lasted well into the night. They'd barely gotten out of bed long enough to enjoy a meal or two. Instead, they'd reveled with awe in their joining, getting to know each other, their guides and good lord above, their bodies.

Rahn's mouth stretched wide in a loud, tired yawn. Quieting his mind, he reached along the bond he shared with Mahpiya. And now Adonei.

"Mah, come to me," he sighed aloud, replete and beyond satisfied.

The sleek corporeal body of the African lioness shimmered into view. And for the first time, Adonei appeared with her. My god, he was a huge cat. His mane was thick and full, a dark chocolate brown that contrasted with his tawny coat. Easily twice as large are Mahpiya, with massive paws, a well-defined chest and eyes the same honey color as Chrys. Adonei stretched out beside his mate. Both of them showed an impressive set of canines as they dropped their jaws and half yawned, half roared rather loudly. Obviously, they were all bone-deep tired.

After the initial joining, Adonei and Mahpiya had given him and Chrys some privacy. If their sleepy demeanors were any indication, they hadn't cut out so they could go to bed early.

"Well, Mah, I would ask why you didn't wake me when Chrys left the apartment, but it's obvious you were sleeping on the job," Rahn chuckled.

Mahpiya sniffed indignantly. Adonei licked his paws.

"Either of you know where my mate is?"

Of course we know where she is, Adonei replied. *Yet even a fully grown lion cannot manage to keep her in one spot.* He swung his huge head toward Mahpiya and said, *Perhaps her mate will be more successful than her spirit guide.*

Sarcasm colored every word. Rahn laughed outright. Chrys would do what she damned well pleased, mated, guided, or not.

Up and headed toward the master bathroom in Chrys' suite, Rahn inhaled deeply. Her scent was everywhere—on the towels, in the air. And all over his skin.

He looked back over his shoulder and motioned to the two lions lying lazily on the floor across the room.

"Come on, you two. While I shower, you can fill me in on what Chrys is up to, as well as what to expect now that we're mated. I can't hear her in my head, but I can hear the both of you well enough."

Mahpiya padded after him.

It is the same with Chrysalyn. The bonds are fully formed, but they do not create telepathic abilities in humans.Chrysalyn can hear and see both Adonei and me. She can see anything we wish to show her, but she cannot hear you, nor you her.

"That makes sense," Rahn replied. Grabbing a washcloth off the rack, he inhaled the feminine scent of his woman before he lathered up with whatever soap she had in the shower. It smelled a bit girly, but he didn't care. Anything that reminded him of his Chrys was just fine with him. Anyone who had a problem with it could kiss the end of his fist.

"So where is she?"

Chrysalyn has gone ashore. She is on a tour of Ibiza.

So they'd reached the Balearic Islands during the night. Damn it, he didn't like the idea of her venturing out alone with a murderer on the loose. The woman could probably take down the culprit, but that wasn't the point. She was his to protect.

Sigh. Well, at least he didn't have to do it alone.

"Can the two of you keep an eye on her? One of you stay with her while the other scouts ahead of her? Keep her out of trouble while I do a bit of snooping. Captain Laurens has a lead for me. I need to check it out without worrying about running into Chrys on the island."

And what of you? Mahpiya asked, her tone abrupt. Obviously, she didn't like the idea of Rahn going about his duties with no one to watch his back.

"I'll be fine, Mah. I'll call if I need you. But what I need more is for you to keep Chrys far away from me while I'm scouting. Hell, even if she's with that Eden asshole, at least she won't be alone."

Adonei jumped to his feet and looked as if he wanted to pounce on Rahn. The lion's snarl was so ferocious, Rahn almost took a few steps back. But he was there to aid and assist, not attack.

But then again, he'd felt Mahpiya's sharp claws across his ass on more than one occasion. Usually right after he'd done something stupid. Hmm, he might have to rethink this whole spirit guide thing with Adonei in the mix. His female cat could get away with swatting him on the backside, but there was no way in hell he was going to let a fully grown, big-assed male do the same. Not without a fight.

Turning off the shower, he toweled off quickly and strode naked through the living room, heading for the closet in the guestroom suite.

Stifling a chuckle, he asked, "Problem with the Eden asshole, Adonei?"

I do not care for the human. But he said nothing more.

"Chrys may be stubborn, but she'll listen to you if she's in danger. She'd better or I'll have to paddle her ass. Go join her on her tour, all right? Tell her I said good morning and I'll catch up with her for dinner."

With that, the air around the two majestic beasts shimmered and shifted until they faded before his eyes. With their essence still vaguely present in his head, Rahn dressed, grabbed a quick bite then headed to the ship's bridge to see Captain Laurens.

CHAPTER TEN

Chrys forced her eyeballs to remain uncrossed as the tour guide's deep monotone droned on, and on.

"Welcome to Ibiza. Third in size of Spain's Balearic Islands, Ibiza's charms include a magnificent bay that rivals that of Naples. There's also a chain of golden beaches and an ancient and picturesque main town. As much a colony of discerning artists and writers as it is a popular tourist destination, Ibiza still offers many areas of charm, tranquility and stunning natural beauty…"

Blah, blah, blah.

Adonei stalked into her head. About damned time.

'Adonei, where in the world have you been?' she scolded.

Getting to know your mate. He sends a good morning greeting and looks forward to your company for supper.

Immediately, sweet warmth infused her soul and brought a smile to her lips. Her mate had sent her a message, even though she'd snuck out of bed this morning. Her mate—amazing how two simple words could be so soothing, yet conjure the most wicked images in mind, like the fierce loving of the previous night. There'd been such an urgency to be mounted, stroked inside and out, that she'd lost her mind under a barrage of feeling. The depth of hunger sunk so deep, it had sent her emotions reeling. Even now, it was almost too much to fathom.

A tremor snaked through her body. Her temperature soared while her stomach tripped. Ears burning, Chrys wondered how long it'd been since she'd actually blushed from thinking about a man. Rahn. God, he simply had her undone.

"Damn it," she muttered to herself. Her head had been so wrapped up in the man, she'd missed a step and stubbed the hell out of her toe. Guess sandals weren't ideal for sightseeing in the old medieval stone pirate towers of the island.

Okay, time to get a handle on herself.

The tour guide's dull voice intruded once more.

"Ibiza and Formentera have been a popular destination for visitors from overseas for thousands of years, but unfortunately it is only during the last few decades that these frequent visitors have brought money with them on their visits to the islands."

Hardy har har. Chrys winced at the dry humor.

'I am bored out of my head. I think I'll go off on my own,' Chrys whispered along her link with her lions. Strange how Mahpiya occupied the same space now, yet the feline was separate and apart from her awareness of Adonei. Almost like they had their own special connection without excluding "the guys".

Chrysalyn, it is not wise to venture off alone, the lioness said firmly.

Apprehension snaked through the link and Chrys felt compelled to listen to the big cat and do exactly as she suggested. She pushed the strange feelings away.

'I've got two bad-assed African lions with me. What do I possibly have to be afraid of?'

The uneasiness of the previous moment surged into full-blown protective instinct. Mahpiya was concerned for her. But why?

'May I call you Mah, like Rahn does?' she asked respectfully.

Of course.

'Thank you. Now, Mah, what's going on? I can feel you're on full hunter alert. And shouldn't one of you be with Rahn?'

Neither lion said a word for what felt like eons. Their postures seemed easy enough, but tension wrapped around the bond like a tangible thing. They were hiding something. But if Mahpiya was anything like Adonei, no amount of harping in the world would get her to spill.

Sigh. Well, perhaps she'd try anyway. Even picking away at the patience of a spirit guide had to be less boring than this stupid tour she'd signed up for.

'Well, since neither of you are telling, I guess I'll drop it.' For now. 'Meanwhile, let's go into the heart of town and explore. Maybe get some lunch.' Chrys didn't wait for them to answer or give permission. With a farewell wave to an older couple she'd met while debarking off the ship, she turned and left the droning tour guide and the group of tourists behind her.

Down the road was a row of modern restaurants and shops, all top-notch according to her research. There was one that specialized in rare gifts. Oooh, and they carried Dominican Republic hand-rolled cigars. Wow. Would Rahn enjoy something like this? He'd never smoked in her presence, but a man of such impeccable taste might appreciate a seasoned mild cigar. For her, there was nothing better than a Tatiana groovy-flavored smoke with an after-dinner dessert. Or the coffee-flavored smoke of a Kahlua cigar mixed with the cool smoothness of a cream-laced beverage. Yum.

With her purchases tucked into her day bag, Chrys walked up a hill, turned down a quiet street and settled for a small mom-and-pop cafe for lunch. Suppressing laughter at Mah and Adonei's antics, she stepped through the door and was immediately shown to a table out back with a clear view of the sea's crystal blue waters off in the distance.

The food was fabulous. She'd never been a big fan of Mediterranean food, but this stuff was wonderful. With every kind of cuisine under the sun to choose from, perhaps the French five-star restaurant down the street would get a visit before she headed back to the ship later. After all, Ibiza was no backwater island, but a place where the young and chic came to vacation.

Her companions were quite a pair. The faint image of the two lions grooming each other lovingly as she sipped a cup of espresso produced an inward smile. Then the next instant, Mah swatted at Adonei's head after he'd said something so totally male even Chrys grimaced. The lioness was quick-witted and even quicker with her claws. And, of course, Chrys had to throw in her two cents, usually on Mah's side. Soon Adonei was mumbling about catty women who were too smart for their own good, and perhaps he would go and keep Rahn company after all. Chrys bit the inside of her cheek and tried to keep her mirth under wraps—not smart to have the locals thinking she'd gone bonkers by laughing at someone they couldn't see.

After lunch, she stepped out into the bright afternoon sunshine. The sun was dazzling, shining off the many white stone churches common in every town on the island.

Then the hairs on the back of her neck hit orbit, standing on end as the bottom fell out of her stomach. Someone was watching her.

After waltzing around the island with no set destination, Chrys had no idea how far away or where her nearest shipmates were hanging out. Yep, it was times like this she sure as hell appreciated having a spirit guide. Correction—two spirit guides.

At the first twang of apprehension, both Adonei and Mah bolted up into sitting positions, ears pricked forward. Adonei's presence faded and she knew he'd gone to investigate what, or rather who, was both ahead and behind her. There was no doubt that in the second she stood in front of the eatery, pretending to explore the beautiful potted plants, Adonei had scoped out each possible route in and out of the area as well as surveyed every person in close proximity.

Meanwhile, Mah's calm power-infused presence radiated down their newly formed bond. Someone might be tailing her, but she sure as hell wasn't alone. Far from helpless, Chrys readied herself, reached for and caught the calm focus required to quickly measure and take down an enemy.

The air off to her left rippled in waves just before Adonei's huge corporeal form shimmered into view. Mahpiya remained out of sight, but clearly visible in her mind's eye.

You are indeed being hunted.

Hunted? Who would dare?

It is the Eden person. I do not like it.

'Well, that sure as hell makes two of us,' she hissed back. Why would Eden be tailing her? He'd always appeared to be so nice and gentlemanly. Not to mention damned good-looking. Did he really mean her ill? Perhaps Adonei was simply overreacting. Or, as usual, he'd been correct in his first assessment of the man.

Well, time to find out.

'Adonei, please lend me your senses.'

Immediately, eyesight and hearing sharpened. Natural ability increased many times over as every cell was infused with the lion's raw power. Taking her time, Chrys and her two invisible escorts turned down a narrow road and out onto the main boulevard.

Eden was a good enough distance away that a typical person wouldn't have noticed his presence. The man was awfully good at tailing, which meant only one of three things—she and Adonei were both paranoid, Eden was a bad guy or he was a special ops person like herself. Odds on that first one were highly doubtful and the thought of him being either of the other two sent a chill up her spine.

She kept moving. With her enhanced senses, not only did Chrys catch the musky scent of his body, but she could have heard his soft footsteps a mile away.

Then, as suddenly as she'd sensed Eden behind her, he was gone. Only to be replaced by the presence of another man she hadn't expected to run into.

Rahn was across the wide boulevard. He stalked—it was the only word she could think of to describe the graceful and dangerous way the gorgeous man moved—down the stairs of what appeared to be the town hall and headed her way.

Two men were at his side. One was a local cop. In her line of work, she could spot a government gofer a mile away, even if he was dressed casually in cargo pants and a button-down shirt. The other man, taller than Rahn, but not nearly as well-built, was none other than the captain of the ship. So what was Rahn doing with these people? His case was supposed to be in Rome, not on Ibiza.

'What the hell is Rahn up to? I'd recognize that I'm-on-duty look anywhere.'

Not expecting either cat to actually tell on the man, Chrys ducked into the nearest shop and waited for him to pass by.

This direction headed right for a crowded town market her tour group had passed earlier. If she was careful, it would be the perfect place to tail him without being noticed. She hoped. After all, Rahn wasn't one of the most distinguished undercover specialists in her unit for nothing. But she was damned good at her job too. And at the rate the men were walking they'd passed by now.

Chrys stepped out into the street on silent feet.

And ran right into Rahn's chest.

"Chrys?"

She watched the expressions on his deeply tanned face morph from surprise to understanding to flat-out pissed off. His jaw tightened and ticced. The lips that had kissed her so wonderfully every day and night now pulled back in a snarl, baring sharp white teeth.

Shit. So much for following him at a discreet distance.

"What the fuck are you doing up here by yourself?" he growled quietly. One look at his face and the men accompanying him gave sympathetic smiles and got the hell out of Dodge. The man looked like a volcano.

"Woman, get your ass back to the ship right fucking now. Better yet, I'll take you my damned self." He grabbed her by the hand and practically dragged her down the hill.

What the hell was going on? She didn't think she'd ever seen Rahn so angry. Not even after the time he'd been shot in the ass by a bad guy while diving for cover in the middle of a shootout.

And who the fuck did he think he was talking to? She was a grown woman who didn't require nor allow a babysitter.

"Slow the hell down or let go of my damned hand," she snapped. "I'm wearing sandals, not running shoes."

His answer was a grumble she couldn't quite make out. Sounded something like having to get his woman back where she belonged?

Well, my mate, shall we leave these two alone for a time? Adonei asked Mahpiya. His tongue lolled out of the side of his mouth and Chrys could have sworn he was grinning. With that, his corporeal form vanished and his presence dimmed. Mahpiya disappeared all together.

Damned cats.

* * * * *

Eden bit back an eager grin. His thoughts were fixed on the beautiful prize of a woman walking ahead of him. Chrysalyn's smooth caramel skin glistened with a light sheen along her shapely calves. His mouth watered at the strong compulsion to taste the crease at the back of her knee to confirm the moisture was a film of sweat mixed with the tangy humidity of the island.

Chrys called to him—mind, body and soul. She was only a short distance away now, barely a block. If he could get to her before she reached the town square, he'd have a chance to, uh, persuade her to spend a bit of quality time with him before it was time to return to the ship to leave port.

Eden wasn't sure why, but just as he was about to pass the steps of the town hall, he came to a halting stop and stayed put, just out of sight.

Seconds later, the Rahn asshole came down those steps accompanied by a local cop he recognized from his last trip through here, along with the captain of their ship.

His pharaoh hadn't said anything about peace officers, captains or assholes in her interpretation of the upside-down Empress card. And if both the Rahn person and Chrys were in this very same spot, did that mean they were here in port together? As a couple? No, not possible. According to the cards, Chrys was supposed to have lost interest in Rahn and leaning toward him instead. Hmm. He'd have to have a talk with his lovely tarot reader when he made it back to the ship.

Risking a peek out of the little alcove he'd ducked into, Eden watched the Rahn asshole rake his hands through his hair. At this angle, the man reminded Eden of one of his own cousins. A strong chin, even stronger body, deeply tanned skin. An air of nobility and honor clung to him like a second skin. His stance screamed royalty. Just like himself.

Listening intently, Eden's spine stiffened at the words of the three men who stood talking on the steps. His lungs seized as if they were afraid to breathe. Heart kicked up into a wild rhythm. Stomach twisted into a sick knot.

Eden's Catalan language skills were somewhat rusty, but he recognized the words "dead" and "killer" in any language.

The Rahn asshole's jaw clenched tight as he questioned the peace officer. "The woman found early this morning.

Same description? Same type of wounds?"

"Yes, sir. She was found just after the ship pulled into port. Wealthy female, Caucasian, blonde hair. Not a resident of the island. A visitor…"

"Who didn't come here on our ship," Rahn interrupted. "Naked and bound, but other than the knife wounds, she was untouched. No rape, no assault. Damn it, just like the others."

Eden pressed closer against the wall between him and the other men.

"Anyone else know about this?" Rahn asked quietly.

The captain of their vessel replied. "Absolutely not. I've spoken to all of the officials in every port we've touched. They've all agreed to let your agency handle the situation."

Agency, eh? So the Rahn asshole was some kind of high-up law dog? And if he worked with Chrys, did that mean she was a cop too? Eden backed up the way he'd come and took the long way around back to the ship. His harem mistress needed a talking-to. And he obviously needed a change of plans.

* * * * *

Rahn was practically on her ass as they both stormed through the door into their apartment. She rounded on him, her face lined with confusion and her fist jammed into her hip.

"Rahn, what the hell are you so upset about?"

The image of his beautiful mate flashed into his mind. She lay in a crumpled, bloody heap, her lifeless eyes glazed over, seeing nothing. The woman they'd found earlier could have easily been Chrys. Just the thought of not having her at his side sent a rush of heated fury through his soul. He teetered dangerously close to the edge of sanity just now. Simply couldn't handle losing her. Not again.

"Damn it, Chrysalyn, how the hell can I protect you if I can't manage to keep your ass where you belong and away from danger?" he yelled.

Yelled? He never yelled. The wide bug-eyed shock on Chrysalyn's flushed, but lovely, face was enough to embarrass him down to his toes. He took a step back, appalled by his own behavior. Didn't last long, considering there was a murderer on the loose and she was prize pickings.

Sobering quickly, he snapped his mouth shut, knowing the wheels of her agile mind hummed from the implication of his words. Damn, he couldn't believe what he'd just let slip. And Chrys wouldn't forget it. In fact, the woman was probably weighing the importance of each word he'd just said.

But instead of giving him the argument he expected, she turned to duck into the sanctuary of her bedroom.

He wasn't having it. Anger flared. Control didn't seem to be anywhere near at the moment, which seemed to be the case more and more of late when in her presence.

"Woman, do you hear me talking to you?" Rahn growled, reaching for her. He had to feel her, had to hold her in his arms. A deft pop of her knuckle in just the right spot had his muscled forearm numb in seconds.

"Yeah, I heard you all right. How could I not? And keep your damned hands off me."

"What? Well, you haven't seemed to mind my hands on you every night we've met up in bed." Ouch. He hadn't meant to say that. The hurt look on her face told him she hadn't expected him to, either. "Chrysalyn, baby, I'm sorry. I didn't mean that. It's just…"

"Save it, Mr. Benson."

Aw, hell. She'd called him Mr. Benson. Definitely not a good sign.

"If there's one thing I can't stand is a man who throws something in my face. Someone who takes a special moment and turns it into a guilt-inducing negative," she fumed.

A grumbled "asshole" reached his ears as she stomped

over the threshold of her room and slammed the door in his face. He stood there with his nose pressed against the smooth lacquered wood and tried to gain at least a bit of composure. With a sigh, he sucked down his pride and let the groveling begin.

"Chrysalyn, I'm sorry," he called through the door. "I was just so worried about you, I lost it for a minute. A body was found just this morning, not an hour after we docked."

Her door slid open. Well, he'd gotten her attention, but the flint-hard look in her eyes clearly said he wasn't getting any forgiveness. He prepared to spend a lot of time on his knees making up for this blunder. But god, was she worth it.

Lowering her head, she glared up at him with a "you'd better have a good explanation" look. Damn, she was so sexy. Even more so in her anger. He must be nuts. Raking a hand through his hair, Rahn backed up a step, blew out a frustrated breath and spoke as many words as he could string together. Which weren't many.

"Chrys, you know the position I'm in." He shot forward in just enough time to get his boot wedged into the space between the doorjamb and the open door. "Listen, I'm working. I'm undercover. I lied about going to Rome. My case is right here aboard this ship. We didn't know the danger or what was going on until after Geri sent you here on vacation."

Arms crossed over her tempting bosom, she snapped. "Why didn't she just have me work the case since I was already here?"

"Because you're supposed to be on vacation. If you don't believe me, then call her. But I can't divulge the nature or details of this case without her permission. I'm sorry, sweetheart, as much as I love you, I can't…"

Oh hell. Had he just let that slip too? God, he couldn't seem to keep anything behind his teeth when Chrys was around. Perhaps it was her fierce spirit that kept him off balance. Or the way she gazed at him with those lovely almond-shaped eyes of hers. Or that luscious ass that winked at him every time she walked by. Or her scent. Or…hell, he could go on forever. The list of what he loved about her was simply endless.

"Rahn? Did you say…? No, never mind. It doesn't change the fact that you lied to me. What else did you lie about, huh? Did you just want to get a bit of bedtime distraction while you're working your case, just to disappear from my life again after it's over? Son of a bitch."

Again, he was presented with her back. But there was no way he was letting her go. She might not believe what he said, so he'd just have to give a bit of action to go along with them. He reached out, careful to get her by the wrist so she couldn't do that pressure-point arm-numbing thing on him again.

Instead, he found himself rolling across the floor into her room. His head made contact with the foot of the large platform bed with a thud. And all the air whooshed out of his lungs when a pissed-off sistah landed hard in the middle of his chest.

Thighs spread wide, Chrys sat high up on his pecs. Arms trapped at his sides, the woman used the odd angle of his neck for leverage. A strong thumb pressed into the base of his trachea and delivered a most uncomfortable sensation that made him want to gasp and gag at the same time. He couldn't move without injuring her or himself.

"And I told you to keep your damned hands off me," she growled.

Skirt bunched up around her hips, the subtle scent of her delectable pussy tickled his nose. His cock shot to attention. A lethal agent sat on his chest, a thumb in just the right position to cause his windpipe considerable damage, he couldn't move…and he had a hard-on?

Yep, he was definitely crazy.

CHAPTER ELEVEN

Chrys instinctively eased the pressure off his throat when Rahn gagged. But only a bit.

How dare the idiot bring up their lovemaking. He clearly didn't trust her to walk down the street alone. Then another thought bloomed in her mind—murders. He'd insinuated that they were tied to this ship somehow. They had to be or he wouldn't be as ridiculous about her being off alone when he knew she could take care of herself.

On the other hand, spirit guides for company or not, Rahn had let her waltz around unarmed and unaware of the true danger.

Adonei and Mahpiya stirred in the forefront of her mind for the first time since she and Rahn had literally run into each other on the hip, upbeat avenues of Ibiza. A wisp of thought eased through their bond and she felt like an instant fool.

Trust between her and her mate had nothing to do with this situation. After all, she'd suspected the man had been working a case all along. The rules that applied to Aegis agents, unfortunately, didn't apply to relationships. He wouldn't and couldn't share with her. The more she knew, the more danger she was in. The man was protecting her.

Not to mention following protocol and orders. Just as she would have done had their roles been reversed.

Mahpiya gave her a glimpse of what her man was feeling. A flood of insecurity and heart-seizing fear streaked through their bond. Every emotion she could think of flooded her consciousness, caught up in a tangle of uncertainty, followed by determination and fierce protectiveness—and it was all Rahn's.

Except for this man, no one other than her cousin, Delaine, had ever looked out for her. And he loved her. Sure, it may have slipped, but it didn't change the fact that he'd said it.

This man put every male she'd ever met to shame. Sexy. Fearless. And just a little bit vulnerable. What an arousing combination. Sitting on his chest, their bodies pressed together in this position, she felt every flex and twitch of his rock-hard pecs. The sensitive flesh between her legs gave an answering tremor. Instantly aflame, the roaring heat of desire for Rahn consumed her. With a tone she'd never heard herself use before, Chrys gave him a new set of orders.

"Don't fucking move," Chrys growled. As if he could with his neck at such a wild angle. Chrys removed her thumb from the notch of his throat and settled her hands on the floor on either side of his head. But she was and would remain in charge. She needed to take him, rather than be taken. And he would move when she told him to, damn it.

Rahn flipped her off his chest and pinned her underneath his big body. No way. Wasn't happening. She rolled him off and landed on top again. By the time the dance was done, they were halfway across the room, dizzy, out of breath. And laughing like two loons with carpet burn.

Side by side on the thick rug, their chests heaved and fell from exertion. Turning to look into the other's eyes only resulted in more chuckling. On a dime, Rahn's twinkling, whiskey brown eyes grew smoky, hungry. His jaw tightened along with the intensity of his gaze. That look reached through her clothes, clear down to her soul. It was like lying on the floor with Superman, complete with X-ray vision and sex appeal that stirred up a longing so raw that it had her exploding off the floor again.

Mahpiya's wild roar sounded in her brain. The huntress had come out to play.

And this time, things would be seen through to their rightful conclusion—Rahn naked underneath her with his powerful cock thrusting deep. And loving it.

This time, when she planted herself on top of him, his fingers sank into her hips and held her there. Thighs splayed wide, Chrys scooted up his chest so she could reach his lips. A split second before she slanted her mouth over his, his fingers began to undo her blouse. To hell with niceties or preliminaries. Swatting his hand away, she ripped the damned thing down the middle. Between her and Rahn, they sure seemed to be destroying a lot of clothes lately. Shucky darn.

Buttons flew in all directions, landing around the room with soft thuds, followed by the soft swish of linen as the shirt joined them on the floor.

Screw the skirt.

With the crotch of her little slinky panties pushed aside, Chrys dry-humped the bulge in Rahn's pants. Fumbling for the zipper of his jeans, now damp with her own cream, she almost breathed a sigh of relief when Rahn pushed her hand aside and freed his steel-hard cock.

Damn, could the man get any more perfect? Not only was he built like a six-foot tank covered with perfect tanned skin, but his cock was literally a golden rod. Wide at the base, thickly veined and delicious. And just the perfect length to fill her to bursting without pain.

"Does this mean you forgive me, love?"

"Shut up and fuck me already," she panted. The shaft of his cock brushed the inside of her thighs and scalded.

God, she wanted him.

Hot. Nasty. Rippling pleasure whirled from her soaked pussy around to the nerves at the base of her spine, and back again. The flared head of her lover's staff teased her entrance before sinking inside.

Rahn met her thrust for thrust as her hips slammed frantically, seeking, craving.

"Sssss, yes. More, baby. Please." The wild hunger to mate, to be pumped full of his seed drove her relentlessly toward the pinnacle of climax.

Chrys balanced on the balls of her feet and each plunge of his cock met nothing but pussy. Gaze lowered, her eyes were riveted on the erotic sight of his flesh disappearing inside hers. Hard met soft as Rahn's flushed, marble-hard cock sank into her sopping core with purpose.

She looked up. Rahn's gaze followed hers.

"Damn, baby, you're so wet. Look at all that cream dripping down my cock." He surged into her welcoming body.

She gasped, "All your fault."

Through gritted teeth, he replied, "I'll gladly take the blame for making you so hot and juicy."

She swiveled her hips, forcing a cry from both their throats.

"God, woman, you're going to kill me."

"Yeah, but you'll die a happy, happy man."

In her mind's eye, she couldn't see the fierce mating of their spirit guides. Instead, there was a faint hint of Mahpiya's pleasure as her mate took her ferociously. And that little bit of bliss, the sexual heat generated by both couples, added to the energy of her lovemaking with Rahn and pushed the swelter up a notch, or two. Then three. Good lord!

"My god, do you feel that?" she panted.

"Yes," Rahn hissed in sync with the surge of lust thrumming down their bond. "Oh god, yes."

Strong, slightly roughened fingers wrapped around the

globes of her breasts and weighed and palmed them before gently pinching the diamond-hard nipples. A streak of pleasure-pain sent her pleasure streaking toward the rafters.

"Bite me, Rahn. Please."

He sat up, grabbed her by the hips and raised her body up and down on his cock. At the same time, his lips closed over the sensitive spot where neck met shoulder and bit down.

Rahn's fingers dug into her ass and hips, sending a sensuous zing down the back of her thighs as he pounded her pussy. Teeth and tongue claimed her. His other hand squeezed and teased her nipples. And the untamed feral heat of the spirit guides stampeded through the psychic connection.

Good lord, could she possibly take any more stimulation? Rahn bit down harder. All she could do was be swept along for the ride.

Chrys' whole body stiffened as she came on a strangled cry.

* * * * *

With a receiver in his hand, Rahn moaned helplessly as the hot flick of a wet tongue tormented the base of his balls. That special spot just below his sac, but not quite to the pucker of his ass. Chrys found it during their earlier love play and was clearly determined to drive him out of his bloody mind every chance she got.

He lay on his back, shivering, trying to hold it together. One hand held a secure satellite phone tight to his ear, while the other buried itself down to the scalp of the head moving up and down between his legs.

"Yeah, lick it, baby." The words slipped past his lips before he could catch them.

"Well, damn, I love you too," echoed an amused voice through the earpiece. Shit, he'd been so distracted by the smooth glide of his woman's tongue, he hadn't realized he'd hit the speed dial, and was even less aware of the line ringing.

He covered up the phone and tried to extract his cock from his mate's oh-so-lovely mouth.

"Chrys, baby, I can't think when you do that."

She opened wide, took both his balls into her mouth and gently suckled. Oh, damn.

"Chrys. God, woman, if you don't stop, our boss is gonna hear me come."

Stilling immediately, her lips fell open on a gasp and his sac fell heavy against the inside of his thigh. He'd never seen Chrysalyn blush such a lovely shade of red-infused caramel. If she hadn't looked so mortified, he would have laughed.

With a final swipe of her tongue over the weeping head of his throbbing staff, she crawled up his body, sat up long enough to pull the covers over them, then settled down with her cheek pressed into the crook of his shoulder.

His arm automatically circled her body and pulled her closer until her short silky curls brushed his chest. It tickled. A satisfied sigh escaped her lungs as she settled in. Stray fingers plucked and played with his nipples. The sensation spread out from the taut nubbin across his pecs, only to dive-bomb for his cock. He closed his eyes and prayed.

Lord, please help me to not drop the phone and hump my woman senseless with our boss on the line.

Mahpiya's subtle chuckle sounded in the recesses of his mind.

Geri's amused words blared through the earpiece. "Well, are you back, Rahn?"

"Yeah, boss, I'm back. I'd like to put you on speaker so Chrys can hear too."

"So that's who has you moaning like a moose in heat, eh?"

Rahn hit the speakerphone button and the voice of the woman who'd been more friend than manager to both him and Chrys filled the room.

"Good morning, Chrysalyn."

"Mornin', Geri."

"What's up? How are you?" Geri asked. Even if Rahn had been both deaf and blind, it would have been hard to miss the cheeky sarcasm lacing her words.

"I'm fine. At least I'm not bored. As for what's up…well, Rahn is."

Rahn's mouth fell open.

"Chrys!" Damned woman.

"What?" she queried, then had the nerve to cast him an innocent-as-a-new-kitty stare. "Well, I can't help it if you're sexy as hell."

The two women giggled like schoolgirls at the mall on a boy-watching trip. Rahn felt his cheeks go up in flames. His mind's eye filled with Adonei, who had no problem grinning at his expense. What was this, torment Rahn day or something?

With a gentle pinch to Chrys' gorgeous round ass, he sucked up the embarrassment and chuckled along with the ladies. Besides, he was too damned sated and happy to stay upset over his woman bragging about his cock. There were certainly worse things she could have said.

Giggling up at him with a wicked waggle of her eyebrows, Chrys toyed with him as her hand traveled from his pecs and skated over his twitching abs on a clear path to his still-full rod. Rahn sucked in a wild breath as his stronger grip eased hers back to its semi-harmless position on his chest with a muttered curse.

"Enough, you two. Let's get down to it. Rahn." Geri's tone was all business. "Report."

"Captain Laurens accompanied me into Ibiza to see the local law dogs. And another body was found. Same profile as the others, same description of a possible suspect."

"This is just awful," Chrys whispered with genuine distress.

He met her gaze and frowned with a shake of his head. She wasn't supposed to know anything about his mission.

A certain protocol had to be followed to get what he wanted, regardless of the fact that they lay skin to skin.

Geri overheard her quiet anguish anyway.

"Chrys, what do you know about what Rahn is doing?"

"Well, the man constantly fusses at me for doing what I always do, which is take care of myself. Then there's all the growling he does whenever I'm with my friend, this really good-looking man named Eden..."

Rahn's entire body stiffened involuntarily. Mahpiya's and Adonei's growls joined his. Just the mention of the man's name irked him. Irked all of them, except Chrys.

"Geri, with Chrys so close to danger, I request permission to brief her on my current case. She doesn't need to take part in any of the activities or investigation, but I'd be much more comfortable if she were in the know."

"I agree," Geri replied.

Chrys pushed up on her elbow and glared at him. "Well, I don't."

"What?"

She narrowed her eyes and snapped, "I said, I don't agree."

The woman would choose now to be stubborn. Rahn gritted his teeth as she explained.

"I'm a trained professional with the same clearance as you. I'm on vacation, not inept."

"Yes, and on vacation means no work. It's my job to see to your safety, mate."

"Mate?"

Geri's question went ignored as Rahn's irritation flared. Did the woman always have to be so difficult? A few choice curses colored the air and aura about them to a few shades of blue as she plowed on.

"Look, Rahn, you may as well stop trying to use this mate business to put me on lockdown. I'm not some soft flower that needs protecting any more than you are. I'll walk and work by your side or not at all."

"What?" Rahn's brows snapped down into a frown. "Are you threatening me, woman?"

"Look, this isn't up for debate," Chrys continued.

Geri stepped into the fray with a chuckled sigh.

"Here's the skinny, Chrys. For the past year, there's been a murder near every port that ship has traveled to. All of the victims were similar in regard to their stations in life, though their physical profiles differed. The last four or five incidents, witnesses have provided a partial description of a possible suspect. Always the same, a man dressed in all black who walked with distinction and a certain presence. Medium height and build. Hell, could be anybody."

"And," Rahn chimed in, "just because this ship is full of nothing but privately owned, high-end, multimillion-dollar condos and wealthy people doesn't mean the killer isn't one of them."

Surprisingly, Chrys didn't say anything. But with every port they passed, the unsolved mystery brought with it a smothering oppression that sat heavy on Rahn's shoulders. Made him wish he could skip this investigation all together, shadow Chrys off the ship and go back home to London. Even if he had to truss her up like a turkey and toss her into a sack to do it. But it simply wasn't an option.

Last night the ship had moved back into open sea. In no time they'd be pulling into the port in Athens with only two more ports-of-call until they reached Alexandria. And for some reason he couldn't quite fathom, the closer they got to Egypt, the more concerned he became.

CHAPTER TWELVE

No fucking like bunnies—or in their case, lions—in the hot tub. No cuddly kisses and sweet words with breakfast in bed. Mr. Romance was nowhere to be found.

In his place was some tyrant Chrys wanted to skewer. Since when was Rahn all business this early in the damned morning? She was supposed to be on vacation, damn it. Not dragged out of bed in time to meet the sun coming up over the horizon. Even if the view was brilliant.

Chrys stood in her room at the glass doors, gazing toward Athens. Greece, garden of gods and kings. Ancient. Unique. Beautiful. And too fucking bright. The terra-cotta buildings plastered with sparkling white façades reflected the light of the sun so brightly it was like staring directly at the largest star in the solar system. Chrys closed her eyes and watched myriad orange-white sparkles dance against the black backdrop of her eyelids. Even if she did crawl back into bed, she'd never get back to sleep now.

Dragging herself away from the deck doors, she snatched the curtain closed and stomped into the oversized bathroom for a quick shower. Rahn hadn't told her where they were going or what he was up to, only that they weren't going ashore. So, if they weren't going anywhere, why the hell did he wake her up so early? And why had he left workout clothes on the bed for her? And where the hell was the man, anyway?

It would have been so simple to ask Adonei. But she just didn't feel like bothering with anything male, whether spiritual or logical, right now.

Dressed, and grumpy enough to growl obscenities at her hairbrush, Chrys pulled the hood of her sweatshirt up over her non-cooperating bed head, slipped on her tennis shoes and socks and headed for the kitchen. No Rahn, but the distant sound of running water and the steaming plate of food sitting on the dining room table answered at least a couple of her questions. He'd cooked breakfast for her before jumping in the shower. How sweet.

Didn't do a damned thing for her mood.

Instead of the cholesterol-laden, high-fat meal she craved, there was a light breakfast of two slices—two little measly slices—of smoked bacon and a boiled egg. Her spirits lifted a bit when she spotted the wheat toast with a smattering of butter and her favorite peach preserves. One bite had her sighing with pleasure. That and a cup of gourmet coffee to die for, with just the right amount of cream and sugar.

Wait, back up. How did Rahn know she loved peach preserves?

Of course my Adonei told him. There isn't much those two don't discuss these days, came Mahpiya's sultry voice floating into her head. An image of the regal cat appeared in her mind. Her golden fur shimmered, slightly translucent as Mah settled back on her haunches and licked a paw.

'Those two sit up and talk about me?' Chrys inwardly gawked around a bit of the heaven-covered toast.

Mahpiya's lack of response, in addition to a "duh" expression, told Chrys all she needed to know.

Aloud, Chrys asked, "Well, what else do they say about me and how much detail are we talking here? So, Rahn knows I adore peach preserves. Does the man know the color of my favorite underwear too?"

My child, I would not be surprised if you found a few dozen new pair of said underwear in your size and your three most favorite colors. After all, Rahn has plans for each pair. Strange, each scheme seems to end with the scraps of cloth either in shreds or perched on top of his head...with you still in them. Hmm. His lack of finesse where you are concerned is somewhat comical.

Chrys sputtered and her coffee projected itself a foot across the top of the lovely lacquered table.

Sensing her distress through Mah, Rahn flew out of the room that had served as his former bedroom—these days all he kept in there were his clothes. In a few fleet steps, he was across the living room, through the kitchen and in the dining room, pounding her back with firm, effective whacks.

"Chrys, love, are you all right?"

She just nodded jerkily between lung-wrenching hacks as Mahpiya's smug and totally self-satisfied image faded from behind her eyes.

Excuse me, young Chrys. Adonei is calling to me. With a wink, the damned cat was gone.

Chrys, on the other hand, blushed furiously. With a croaked "I'm all right", she left a concerned Rahn staring after her and hurried to change her coffee-stained t-shirt.

* * * * *

Exactly thirty minutes after Chrys' breakfast, Rahn took his still-grumbling woman down to the fitness area. He'd purposely avoided her questions last night when she'd asked him about heading into port. Most of the owners had gone ashore for an overnight excursion in Athens.

Vacation or not, she needed to keep her skills honed and sharp. The gym was usually reserved for basketball and volleyball, but today the place was all but deserted. They could spar and, if she wished, talk about the case with relative privacy.

Rahn looked her up and down. He loved the way her workout pants hugged her hips and that lovely, lush ass.

The sweatshirt covered up just about everything else, but he knew good and well what was under it—a little gray sports bra. And nothing else.

Before his body could react to the thought of stripping her bare and nibbling on her candy nipples, he pushed the temptation away and focused on the task at hand—sparring.

He dragged her fully into the gym, dropped his gear bag by the nearest wall and squatted to unzip it. Chrys was a petite little thing, but strong in body and character. And he wouldn't go easy on her, knowing the woman would go for blood from the second he signaled "go".

"Name your weapon."

With a roll of her eyes and a sigh, she finally said, "Give me the Japanese bo. For starters."

Her glare spoke volumes. Guess she really wasn't a morning person. Keeping her up half the night exploring every sexual position known to man couldn't possibly have anything to do with her grumpiness.

Rahn dug a pair of bokken out of the bag, tossed her one and walked to the middle of the floor. "On your mark."

Chrys gave a short bow, and it was on.

And damn, the woman was good with the thing. The slim sword-shaped piece of smooth wood sliced through the air with a hiss. A loud clack echoed through the wide-open space as their weapons met. He countered a blow to his upper thigh, but her strike was so hard and solid that the vibration traveled up his arm and settled in the joint between shoulder and collarbone.

A loud "yaaaahhhh" erupted from deep in her being, as if she'd gathered all her chi, all her life force, just for this moment. Three swift kendo blocks warded off his attack, then she flowed into a high diagonal cut, followed by a half-cut, full-cut combination that nearly took his head off.

Chrys signaled a break and took just long enough to strip off her sweatshirt. Then she jumped back into the fray with skill, grace and undisguised intent. Next came a good solid bout of exchanged blows. They both landed several good whacks. No doubt a good soak in the hot tub would be in order later.

With a step back, slightly winded with exertion, Chrys signaled that she was dropping her weapon. But if he thought she was giving in, he was quickly disabused of the notion. Chrys? Quit? Not bloody likely.

The second their weapons clattered to the floor, Chrys left the ground with a flying kick to the torso and landed lightly on her feet. He stumbled backward, quickly regaining his balance. Time to change tactics.

Then again, considering how much had happened in so little time, Chrys must be up to her eyebrows with frustration. Why not let her use this practice time to work it out on him? But he'd better remain focused or she'd pound him into a big greasy spot on the floor.

Chrys stood cool-headed and composed in a perfect horse stance. The perfect fit of her stretchy pants outlined the muscle of strong thighs. Sleek thighs. Delicious thighs. Damn, the woman was hot.

Moving in close, she engaged him in hand to hand with a strange combination of Aikijutsu and Krav Maga. And she gave everything she had, and then some.

Just then he inhaled deeply, trying to catch his breath. And got a whiff of Chrys in all her sweaty glory.

The way the perspiration glistened on her skin called his tongue, urging it to lick a path through it. The ferocity with which she defended and attacked turned him on like nothing else.

This was fucking ridiculous. Even in a fight, he wanted to make love with her. He backed up, trying to ignore the uncomfortable ridge pushing at the front of his sweats. Good thing he wasn't wearing boxers or he'd have a tent in his pants.

A surge of plain old lust swept him from toes to nose. When Chrys let a punch fly for his jaw, he caught her little fist in his larger one and yanked her to his chest, then flipped her around.

His cock pressed into the crack of her ass. She tilted her head and tried to look back at him.

"Rahn?" The way his name rolled off her lips held just a hint of confusion with a splash of arousal. Enough to push him right over the edge.

An open-mouthed lick across the back of her sweaty neck reduced them both to panting, horny-assed agents.

Turning slightly, whatever she was going to say was cut off in the ferocity of Rahn's kiss. A kiss so blatantly carnal, hell, he even shocked himself by the urgency with which his mouth moved over hers.

In seconds, she was squirming, trying to turn around to circle her arms around his waist and grind the flat of her belly against his hardening cock. Peeling the bottom of her damp sports bra up, her lovely breasts spilled into his hands. He teased, palmed and stroked them until she wriggled. She broke the kiss on a groan, whispering her need.

"Mmmm, oooh…" she panted. Her head rolled to the side and he couldn't resist biting and laving the ultra-sensitive spot where neck met shoulders. A series of wild shudders racked her body and her pants became desperate moans.

"Rahn, baby, I need it. Please…"

And he wanted nothing more than to give it to her. But there was no way in hell they'd make it all the way back to their apartment.

Instead, he straightened her bra, tossed her sweatshirt into his gear bag, then scooped her up in his arms. Headed out of the gym, he didn't set her on her feet until they reached the room he'd spotted at the end of the hall on an earlier trip down here.

From this day forward, whenever Chrys thought about aerobics, her face would blush a shade of caramel apple red every time. He would see to it.

The man's kiss was like rich dark chocolate, potent, rich, a pure aphrodisiac. Better than the best cup of hot cocoa in the morning. Better than fine aged port wine. Better than…than peach preserves!

And it only took ten seconds of his delicious mouth on hers to make her want him so bad she ached with it. Her pussy bloomed, swelled and moistened in anticipation of his lovely cock spreading her open and sinking deep.

A moment of concern intruded when she saw where he carried her. It was the damned aerobics room. Obviously, no one was scheduled to use it today since the shades were all down and most folks had gone to Athens. But still, it was a public-use room.

"Rahn, wait. No way." But her body screamed yes when he set her on her feet and a broad palm kneaded her tingling breasts through her sports bra. Her nipples peaked and stiffened, wanting more. More of his touch. More of his cock pressing against her ass cheeks. More of everything.

The *click* of the door lock echoed around the room. It was just the two of them. In a room with mirror-covered walls.

Care melted like snow underneath a hot July sun. Chrys didn't think she'd ever seen a human being strip so fast. In seconds, Rahn's clothes sat piled at his feet. The raw, hard glint of his whiskey brown eyes reached through her soul and pulled. Hard. Speaking of hard, the man was that, and then some. The muscled peak of one biceps rose and fell as his hand stroked the mouth-watering length of his cock. The other arm reached for and caught her.

From between clenched teeth, his desire spilled from his lips.

"Chrys, damn, I want you so much I'm almost crazy with it. Even without asking Mahpiya to lend me her keen sense of smell, your scent reaches out and grabs me by the gut. I need to fuck you."

Dayum!

What the hell could she say to that, other than "Jump me, now"!

But first, she had to taste him.

Dropping to the floor, her knees landed on the soft pile of clothing. Her lips opened in anticipation of his unique flavor. Mouth wide, eyes closed, Chrys leaned forward, so ready to feel him bumping the back of her throat.

With a squeak, her lids flew upward as her hands grabbed for whatever she could get a hold of. Flipped onto her hands and knees, palms flat on the floor, a stream of cool air flowed against her skin as her pants and a pair of skimpy underwear were peeled down and off. Rahn's warm breath came out in a rush against her ear.

"If you touch me, I'll blow. I'm so hot and hard for you, I just need to get inside. Are you ready, love?"

Boy, was she ever!

No man had ever wanted her so much, needed her so badly. The knowledge alone had her soaking wet, swollen and achy.

The tip of his cock nudged her weeping folds apart. Damn, he was so hot the velvety skin stretched taut over the fat head practically scalded and sent her own temperature soaring. With one surge, he was seated to the hilt with his chest plastered against her back, panting like he'd run a marathon.

Chrys' adrenaline ran so high, it barely registered that she held them both off the floor. The only thing she cared about was...more. Hips squirming uncontrollably, she silently begged for him to put out the fire he'd kindled in her womb. Her flesh tried to hold him inside as he slowly, deliberately withdrew.

"Unggh," came his ragged cry as he slammed back inside. His breath whooshed out of his lungs while hers felt corked up in her chest.

Out.

"Rahn, oh my god."

In.

"Oh, yes!"

Out. Too damned slow.

"Rahn, fuck me, damn it."

Chrys felt her lion rise up and push against the surface of her thoughts like never before. It was more than Adonei's consciousness. It was Adonei in pursuit of Mahpiya.

The entire length of Rahn's rock-hard staff disappeared into her body and triggered an explosion of stars. Light streaked across the back of Chrys' mind as the two majestic beasts pounced and came together like the swirling vortex of a summer storm. Both were hunters. Neither was prey. And the mating of spirits was fierce and beautiful, echoing the maelstrom of emotions streaking along the bond to surround Chrys and her mate.

They cried out together, both caught up and caught off guard by the intense rush of sensation.

"Shit!" came their echoed cries.

Then the man became a literal fucking machine.

Eager for every inch, Chrys' body took over and instinct ruled. Her chest hit the floor, leaving just her ass in the air as she clawed frantically for anything to anchor her. Rahn's fingers dug into her flesh, pulling her hips back to meet each stroke.

"Yes, baby. Give it to me," she gasped.

He moved deeper, harder.

"Is this what you want, Chrys?" The words were gravelly, harsh.

She yelled her response. "Yes!"

"My cock and only mine?"

"God, yes!"

"Then come around my cock, love. Let me feel that sweet pussy milk me. Touch yourself, sweet."

Just as she began to stroke her slick, swollen clit, Chrys turned her head and caught their reflection in the mirror. Hell, she didn't think it was possible to get any more turned on than she already was.

She was wrong.

The sight of Rahn's marble hard girth sinking into her willing flesh, along with the fingers plucking and rubbing her slick, swollen clit sent her out of her mind.

Orgasm gathered low and tingled at the base of her spine. It burst through her entire being—mind, soul and body. Chrys came on a loud wail, with Rahn's roar echoing in her ears.

* * * * *

Eden plopped into the nearest living room chair, panting from the morning's activities. He surveyed the room and sighed. Perhaps he'd taken it a bit too far. A slew of porcelain arms and legs littered the floor in front of the specialized curio cabinet. The beveled panes of glass lay shattered into fine pieces amidst the array of special-ordered shirts, kilts, blouses and trousers. He admired the hand-sewn moccasin still on a dislocated foot.

No. There was no way he'd accept the meaning of the cards. She had to be mistaken. Everyone made mistakes. Even pharaohs, right? Yes, even pharaohs. And like everyone else, pharaohs passed from this plane to the next. And many went before their appointed time. Like this one.

And now who would give him direction?

Perhaps he could guide himself? He'd never possessed the level of skill with the tarot as his harem mistresses. Especially this last one. But now he'd ripped her and all her males to pieces in fury as her words echoed in his head.

She'd claimed the upside-down Empress hadn't meant Chrys was losing interest in the Rahn asshole. In fact, his pharaoh had left important information out of her first readings of the damned card and neglected to tell him that the reading was accurate…if the person who'd consulted the cards was a woman.

In that case, the upside-down card could represent that woman and indicate a partial success in an important area of her life.

But if the person consulting the cards was a man, it could indicate a weakening of the figure of his beloved, either because the man experienced sentiments less intensely, because the sentiments of the woman had weakened or because she felt physically or psychologically distant.

But he'd been operating under the presumption that Chrys was losing interest in the Rahn asshole, not feeling physically distant from Eden himself. Not to mention he'd been feeling distant from his harem mistress for some time now. The cards could have easily meant his disintegrating tie with his now-in-many-pieces beloved.

But then again…

Damn it, he just wasn't sure. And he'd become so enraged when his porcelain beauty revealed the other possibilities of the card's meaning, he'd snapped her neck like a chicken before she could finish the explanation. And now she was gone. Still, her absence was not his concern as much as the possibility that he'd missed something in her interpretation or misunderstood what she had been trying to say.

Sigh.

And it would be months before his next pharaoh was completed. He'd just have to make do until then.

CHAPTER THIRTEEN

"I can't believe you're not ready to go," Chrys teased, moving into the kitchen to turn off the lights.

As she passed, Rahn eased up behind her. He pulled her into his arms, planted a loud smack against her temple and held her tight.

"Not my fault. When Captain Laurens ran into us on the way back from our workout, he said he wanted to speak with me for a few minutes. I couldn't possibly cut the man off mid-sentence when he had such important information to share."

"Mid-sentence?"

A fist balled up on her hip while a foot tapped out a cadence on the hardwood floor. And that foot was dressed in the sexiest damned high-heeled, ankle-wrap sandals he'd ever seen. And her dress? Shit, she was going to dinner in that? A black backless halter affair that molded perfectly to her luscious curves until it hit her waist. From there, it flared out with a little flip that made him want to peek underneath it. Surely it was designed for a midnight interlude on a private deck...with her leaning over the railing with it hiked up over her hips as she wiggled her ass at him.

God, at this rate, he'd never make it to dinner. He shook his head to clear it and returned to a safer, less freaky subject.

"So, the good captain's few minutes turned into almost an hour. But the details he passed to me were good ones. Someone got a decent look at our suspect."

"What? That's great news." She turned in his arms and hugged him around the waist. Pushing away, she headed into the dining room and snapped off the light. Rahn trailed behind her, watching her check and double-check that each light was turned off.

"Still annoyed I'm not ready and dressed for our dinner date?"

"Me? Annoyed? Never," Chrys laughed playfully. "Now hurry up and shower already. Every owner I've spoken to has complained about how hard it is to get reservations for this place, and we own the whole damned boat. Our seating time is 8:00 p.m."

"What time is it now?"

The roll of her eyes should have answered the question clearly. "It's 7:58 p.m., sir."

"Well, why don't you go on ahead? I'll meet you downstairs at the restaurant. The fancy highfalutin Japanese one, right?"

"Yep, that's the one." She still moved around the apartment in an endless stride. Now she was checking the locks on the glass doors that led to the deck.

"Hey, I turned on the shower for you already. Move it, handsome," Chrys called from across the expanse of the den and disappeared into his old bedroom, now termed the "guestroom", to complete the security check. He couldn't blame her. If she hadn't done it, he would have. In their line of work, it became second nature after a while, almost a nightly ritual of sorts.

Shucking his clothes on the way to the master bath, Rahn couldn't ignore the sense of foreboding that rode him like a damned cowboy rode a bucking bronco. He simply couldn't shake it.

Mah, go with Chrys and your mate to the restaurant. I'll shower quickly and meet you in about ten minutes.

Mahpiya's presence dimmed. Chrys' giggle from the living room told him that she and Mah were probably teasing the hell out of poor Adonei about something or another.

Males. They just couldn't get a break. And god help them when the two women got together and ganged up on them. Witty, smart. Damned merciless. And he wouldn't have them any other way.

Soothing hot water felt good sluicing over his sore muscles. He and Chrys had sparred every day for the last three days that the ship had been in port in Greece. The woman packed a wallop and gave as good as she got. If he'd had time, he would have rather soaked in the hot tub to loosen up the tense muscles and soothe the knots and bruises up and down his back. The woman had really worked him over. He'd taken it easy on her, but Rahn was sure there were a few choice spots where she could stand a soak.

He was soaping up when Chrys walked in. Neatly arranged on a set of hangers were his favorite suit and a shirt-tie combination that matched her dress. She headed straight to the closet and hung it up. On her way out, she stopped, did a double take then backed up five steps.

"Dayum! You look so yummy." She slid her fingers over the glass, leaving trails across the steam-covered glass. "Too bad the Mastersens are meeting us for dinner, otherwise…"

The words hung in the air as those same fingers teased over the swell of her breasts, as her little pink tongue peeked at him from the corner of her mouth.

Heat crept up Rahn's neck, and it wasn't from the shower. When the woman touched herself like that, said things like that, he couldn't help but feel…well, flattered. Nobody affected him like Chrys. No one could make him feel sexy, cherished and wanted like she did.

"Well, that's all right," she sighed dramatically. "I'll get mine later. On top."

His cock shot to attention.

She grinned and practically skipped from the bathroom. "See you in ten minutes."

Damned tease. But she was his damned tease.

A few minutes later, he stepped out of the shower and stood for a moment, breathing in the thick humid air. Chrys had left the bathroom door open, but her scent lingered. It never ceased to amaze him what a simple whiff of the woman did to his nervous system. His poor cock should be crying out for mercy by now, rather than begging him to call her on her cell and tell her they were having dinner in bed.

Drying quickly, he ducked into the cedar-lined walk-in closet. A smile kicked up one side of his mouth when he saw the underwear and socks sitting perfectly folded on the shelf for him.

She was such a neat freak. Good thing she didn't expect him to be one.

He'd just zipped up his pants when a faint rustle caught his attention. Chrys must have forgotten something.

Rahn walked out of the closet. His stocking feet touched the steam-dampened tile of the bath area when he met pain so intense, the breath froze in his throat. The muscles of his back seized and twitched. From behind, cold steel twisted and plunged deep into his body, separating his ribs to pierce the organs underneath.

And he knew he was a dead man.

* * * * *

With a smile at the light banter going on in her head, Chrys followed an immaculately clean waiter through the restaurant. Rice paper lanterns sent a gentle glow from the center of each large circular table. Japanese kanji symbols strategically placed along the walls and the rich red cinnabar ornaments here and there, gave a feeling of "rightness" to the atmosphere. She wasn't really into Feng Shui, and doubted the decorators of this Japanese restaurant were either, considering the art was of Chinese origins. Either way, her spirit guides seemed to love the energy of the place.

Chrys settled down in her chair, sat back and allowed a sense of peace and relaxation to envelop her—something she hadn't felt since she learned of the case Rahn was working.

The Mastersens were seated and already sipping on frozen, delicious-looking green cocktails. Several couples Chrys didn't recognize were in the middle of ordering the same thing when Mrs. Mastersen spoke to her.

"Chrysalyn, dear," Mrs. Matersen beamed. "I'm so glad you could join us for dinner. You must try one of these. It's a Midori Sunrise and tastes like tropical paradise."

Mrs. Mastersen was an all-out chatterbox. On the way back aboard ship on Ibiza, the woman had amused Chrys when she'd spotted the bag of specialty cigars she'd purchased. She'd introduced herself and her husband, then asked to try one without an ounce of shame. Gray-haired, feisty and carefree, the two were enjoying their retired years sailing around the world. Chrys had loved them on sight.

"Your dress is downright sexy, young lady. Now where is that delightfully handsome beau of yours? And he let you out looking like that? He'd better be careful or Harold here might put the moves on you. Mr. Mastersen was quite the rake in his day. Still has great skill…"

Chrys wondered if the woman had taken a single breath.

"And even after all these years, he still makes sure I come before he does."

Chrys coughed on the iced water she'd been sipping. Way more information than she needed to know. Clearing her throat, a quiet giggle escaped between words.

"Thank you for the compliment on my dress, ma'am.

As for Rahn, an earlier outing took a bit longer than he thought."

Captain Laurens sat down at the head of the table and said, "That would be my fault, I'm afraid. Hope we didn't put too much of a dent in your plans."

Chrys smiled and said, "When I left, Rahn was getting ready. He sends his apologies and should be walking in the door any minute now. So, I think I'll order his drink for him. Waiter?" Chrys called, and another smartly dressed young man headed her way. "I'd like a glass of your best chilled rice wine for my, er, friend. And I'll have one of those green things, please."

"Friend, eh?" Mrs. Mastersen gawked excitedly. "How fabulous for you, my dear. You've dated a while, have you?"

"We've worked together for more than six years and know each other well." The rest of it was none of anyone's business. Out of nowhere, the image of Rahn in the shower burst into her thoughts.

I am sure my charge would blush if he knew what you were thinking just now. Can you think of nothing but his cock?" Mahpiya whispered to Chrys, her tongue lolling to the side.

'Oh, hush up, you. You're not supposed to tell all my secrets, and I can tell from the way the bond feels that Adonei is listening in.'

Of course I am listening in. It is my job, is it not? Adonei sniffed indignantly, then turned to Mah, fussing. *And do you have to speak so boldly regarding your charge's private parts?*

Chrys almost laughed out loud. Didn't he know by now not to set himself up like that? Before she could form a single smart-assed response, Mah was all over him.

My dear Adonei, I believe you are in need of schooling, and given your old age, Mah paused for dramatic effect, *you know I certainly do not have to use the word cock. I have been a spirit guide for eons. There are many other ways to express myself, mate.*

Chrys clamped her lips together, picked up her water

and sipped, trying to hide the smile at the corner of her lips. Oh, boy, here it comes.

I could have called it by some of the other words I have heard over the years, like bacon bazooka…

Bacon what? Adonei queried, his brow pulled down in a confused frown.

Do you not like that word? 'Tis much better than cock, don't you think? No? Perhaps pork sword?

What is it with you and pig meat? Adonei groaned, clearly wishing he hadn't said anything.

Fine. No more pork. So what about tally whacker? Tickle-gizzard? Wanker? Tube steak?

Chrys' own eyebrows flew up at that last one. Tube steak? Eww. Adonei swiped a huge paw at Mah, but the lioness dodged it with a laugh and simply kept right on.

Maypole? Meat whistle? Milk bone? Mr. Happy?

Adonei rolled his eyes and grumbled something about the Great Spirit's sense of humor and boneheaded mates.

Suddenly, the muscled body of the tawny-haired lioness stiffened. Alarm and no small amount of fear streaked down the bond and settled in the pit of Chrys' stomach.

'What? What is it?' Chrys demanded, thinking the lions were upset because Eden was headed their way. The man walked right up to the captain, bowed low and managed, yet again, to insinuate himself into their plans. But it wasn't Eden. It was something else.

Mahpiya's head swung from side to side as if she were looking for something. After a moment or two of soft, seeking roars, her shaken gaze turned inward to Chrys and Adonei. The lioness's answer was laced with undisguised panic. Something Chrys never imagined to see or hear from the great huntress.

My charge! He is gone! I cannot feel or hear him, Mahpiya wailed even as Adonei tried to sooth his distraught mate with broad strokes of his tongue just behind her ear.

Chrys squirmed in her chair in a subdued version of the pee-pee dance. "Excuse me, you all. I need to take a trip to the powder room." Glad no one questioned her, she grabbed her little clutch purse and scooted back from the table, keeping her movements slow and deliberate.

Out in the hallway, Chrys ducked past the entrance to the ladies' room and hurried down the hall, speaking to her spirit guides. She tried to ease Mahpiya, who paced nervously at the forefront of her mind,

It'll be all right. Nothing short of death could take a charge from his spirit guide, Adonei reminded them both.

That's what I am afraid of, Mahpiya screeched.

Adonei nipped the skin just above her shoulder with a muted growl, steel grit behind every word. Mahpiya stilled, startled into a quiet contemplation.

You will cease this negative talk of your charge. Speeding negative thoughts or energy his way will gain you nothing. Come with me, now, he demanded with the quiet authority only an alpha could pull with one so great as Mahpiya.

Before Chrysalyn's eyes, the air in front of her shimmered and blurred as the two big cats took on their corporeal forms. It was the first time Adonei had ever come to her in this form without being summoned. She didn't hesitate.

'Both of you go ahead of me. Find Rahn.'

Adonei turned to Mahpiya and said, *We hunt, my love.*

With a nod of her large regal head, Mahpiya agreed and let out a ground rumbling roar that would have frightened the stoutest heart. They turned and took off in opposite directions.

Walking as quickly as her high-heeled sandals would allow, Chrys moved quietly down the hallways and toward their apartment.

Moments later, Adonei pushed into her mind. What he reported made her strip off her shoes and tuck them under her arm. Her slender fingers dipped down into the front of her dress to retrieve her apartment key as she ran like the wind.

'Oh, no, Rahn. Rahn, don't you dare die, damn it,'

Chrys ordered along the bond with their spirit guides, knowing they would both send her thoughts and feelings along to Rahn the same way they sped his current state to her. He was there, but just barely hanging on to the edge of consciousness. But based on Mahpiya's slight sighs of relief, it was more than there had been when she'd reached out to him mere moments ago.

Chrys burst through the front door, dropping her shoes and purse in the foyer. A quick stop in the kitchen for the first-aid kit, and she was off again, following Adonei's specific directions through the apartment. She knew exactly where to find him—on the master bathroom floor, bare-chested in a pool of his own blood. The tile was so slick with it, she almost skidded as she sped over the threshold. Dropping to her knees, the first-aid kit landed next to his too-still body with a loud clank. The gash in his side bled profusely. Afraid to move him, but knowing she must, Chrys called to the spirit guides waiting to aid her.

Adonei, lend me your strength, she grunted, trying to roll Rahn over on her own.

The lion's brute strength rushed into her muscles, filling them with supernatural might, heightening not only her own strength, but all of her senses as well. The scent of Rahn's blood and freshly showered skin and hair filled her nose and mouth. The sound of his shallow, barely there breathing spilled over her and filled her with an urgency mixed with a strange dose of melancholy.

She pushed it away and focused on the task at hand.

Now able to easily maneuver the dead weight of Rahn's densely muscled body, Chrys gently rolled him to one side and packed the wound with clean linen to staunch the flow of thick, hot, blood. His lids fluttered, but he didn't make a sound.

'Mahpiya, can you nudge him closer to consciousness?'

Chrys knew they had to pull him back to this side of the spiritual plane so he could call Mah. Rahn had to request her help. It was against the spiritual laws for a spirit guide to aid without being asked. They could not impose their will on their charges. But if they didn't do something fast, Rahn would be lost to them. He'd die.

Leaning forward, speaking directly into his ear, Chrys pleaded for him to call to Mahpiya. To ask for her aid, even if he asked with his mind and not his mouth. Rahn's eyes opened for a moment.

"Mah. Help. Please." The words were barely a whisper, but she heard them all the same. The fear that had been riding her released the bands around her heart and allowed it to beat again. Mahpiya's silent relieved response flooded the bond. Rahn would be all right.

Mahpiya disappeared all together from Chrys' consciousness and she knew the lioness focused all her healing energies on Rahn. It was hard work mending flesh and replenishing blood, even for a spirit guide. But she'd saved his life once before. Now she would do it again.

But now Chrys was flat-out pissed off. Someone had done this to her mate. Someone had tried to take Rahn away from her.

Grabbing one of the thick bath sheets off the rack, Chrys covered up Rahn's bloody body and left the bathroom. Not bothering to wipe the blood off her feet or remove her ruined dress, she flew for the nightstand across the huge bedroom. Almost as an afterthought, she spoke to Adonei.

'Guard the apartment, will ya, boy?'

The moment the words left her lips, Adonei's hackles rose. A deep menacing growl rumbled in his chest as his stance took on one of attack, gaze fixed on a point behind her. Chrys went still.

Unease snaked its way down her spine, and the nerves along the bottom of her stomach danced in time with Adonei's growling. But she wasn't afraid. The strength of her spirit guide still flowed like fire through her entire being. Whatever, whoever it was, bring it on.

She turned, ready to drop into a fighting stance if need

be.

"Eden, what the hell are you doing in here?" she demanded. Unsure of his intentions, Chrys instinctively calculated the difference in their body weight and the moves required to take him down fast. He looked slightly crazed, but as soon as the expression appeared, it was gone again.

"Chrysalyn, your dress, what happened? You're covered with blood."

Now he appeared genuinely alarmed. Adonei wasn't buying it, but her man needed help and she didn't have time to deal with this right now. A faint groan caught her attention. Rahn. Heading toward the phone, she tossed the words over her shoulder in a rush.

"Rahn was attacked. He needs a doctor."

"Really? Here?" he gasped. "Go to your friend. I'll get the surgeon and call the local emergency." And Eden was flipping open his cell phone on the way out the door.

Back in the bathroom, she held Rahn's hand, stroked his beautiful fingers and ignored her tears as they splashed on the palm clasped gently in her own.

In mere minutes, Eden was back and the apartment became a hive of frenzied, but calm, activity as the ship's surgeon came in and tried to extract her from Rahn's side. Captain Laurens hauled her out of the bathroom, explaining how both her and Eden's fast thinking had saved her mate. Rahn was placed on a stretcher, covered with blankets and gently lifted from the cold tiled floor. All the while, the ship's doctors, along with the Grecian medics, marveled over the fact he was still alive.

CHAPTER FOURTEEN

The ship was delayed in Greece while a full investigation took place. Nothing. No leads, no suspects. A week and a half later, with the aid of both Mahpiya and Adonei, Rahn was good as new. And while Chrys was relieved, she was so ready to get off the damned ship.

Upon arrival in Alexandria, she was up with the chickens and ready to head ashore. First stop, Qaitbay. Perfect starting point since Rahn was scheduled to meet a contact there anyway. And even better, since she couldn't sit in on that meeting she'd get some much-needed time alone, even if only for an hour.

High up on the imposing limestone walls of the Citadel, the tang of the salty sea air tickled her nose as Chrys took in the beauty literally surrounding her. A crisp breeze off the water took the edge off the midday sun. She raised her face to the sky as it blew over her, ruffling her short curls and cooling her skin from neck to knees.

What a mystical, soul-stirring place. She'd always wanted to see the Sphinx and the Pyramids of Giza. Maybe even the monumental statues of Ramses the Great at Philae. But now that she stood on the banks of the Mediterranean, looking out over the crystal waters, Chrys couldn't believe she'd never looked into coming to Alexandria before.

The sparkling isthmus caught the eye of Alexander the Great more than twenty-three hundred years ago. Founded in 332 B.C., the city still carried his name, though Cleopatra, the last queen of Egypt who happened to be Greek, ruled her kingdom from here during the first century B.C.

Amazing was this fortress built by Sultan Qaitbay in the 1480s. Erected on the very foundation of the famed queen's Lighthouse of Pharos, one of the seven wonders of the ancient world. She wondered what Cleopatra looked like. Imagined the queen spending the night in her lover's arms as they gazed out to the sea toward Rome together, planning, dreaming of a life together.

But Julius Caesar and Cleopatra's love wasn't enough to save them from their own stupidity or the ill wishes of others.

And now Chrys was here with her own warrior lover. A lover who'd recently been nearly gutted.

The same foreboding she'd experienced in Ibiza and the night Rahn was stabbed slithered over her skin. The possibilities tumbled end over end through her mind. True, the attack on Rahn didn't fit the profile of the bad guy he was after. But what if the intrusion wasn't random, like Rahn, Geri and the others speculated?

As soon as the thoughts formed, she pushed them away. She hadn't survived as an undercover agent this long by allowing her life to be ruled by fear. Besides Rahn worried enough for the both of them.

Her thoughts turned toward home. Just where would that be for her when all of this was over? Lately, Rahn had been too busy luxuriating in her more-than-willing body to discuss it.

Do not blame your mate, Adonei complained. *It is not as if you have tried so very hard to speak to him about it.By the way, he expects you to remain where he left you, up on the wall.*

Males. They sure stuck together…which, of course, had nothing to do with whether she was right or wrong. Nor did it matter that she hadn't pressed the issue out of simple self-preservation of her tender heart. Skip it, they'd get around to it.

Shielding her eyes, she looked to the south toward a stone-enclosed harbor so large it resembled a sea full of boats, yachts and ships of various sizes, small to gigantic. To the north was the blue jewel of the Mediterranean. She gazed up to the main building, soaring seventeen meters skyward. When lookouts were stationed here, they could spot invaders an entire day's journey out to sea. On a clear day, perhaps she could see all the way to the Greek isle of Crete.

And this truly was a fortress, complete with inner and outer walls, gardens, courtyards and the towered fort of Qaitbay itself. No wonder it was referred to as the pearl of the Mediterranean.

Wandering around the impressive structure, she found her way to some of the coastal tunnels and passages under the walls that looked more like cave entrances. Thankful for the small windows set at intervals along the way that looked out to sea, Chrys wound her way around and through the dimly lit halls under the structure.

"Huh. Interesting," she mumbled to herself as she huffed and puffed her way up the steepest flight of stairs in all creation. Thankful she was in halfway decent shape, her journey ended—well, almost ended—on the first floor of the famous Qaitbay Citadel's main building.

There was no way in hell she was going to even attempt finding her way through the long, though interesting, passages. She'd just have to find Rahn from here. Better yet, she had two spirit guides watching her back. One of them would just have to go get him. As for Chrys, she was determined to sit her butt down in a chair and enjoy the silent company of the guards looking after the place.

Better yet, she was sure she'd spotted a bustling bazaar

on the way here. Nothing like a good bout of shopping to get a girl back in a good mood.

Interrupting a heated debate between Mah and Adonei about the importance of post-sex conversation, she passed a thought to her companions.

'Adonei, let Rahn know where I am, will ya?'

He is already aware and nearing.

Then to the guards, she said in perfect Arabic, "Excuse me."

They eyed her askance, probably because she was an unescorted female. But these men would respect strength in a woman, even a foreign one. Motioning in the direction she wished to go, the bell sleeve of her white linen blouse fell back a bit to reveal taut skin stretched over well-honed biceps as she firmly, but respectfully, stated her request.

"Can you please assist me in the proper direction to hire a *hantour* to take me to the bazaar?"

One of the men passed a friendly smile, but before he could open his mouth, a stern-faced Rahn stood at her side. The soldier's smile became a full-blown grin.

"Sir, how good it is to see you again. It has been a long time."

Rahn gave the guard a slight bow and extended his arm to a gawking Chrysalyn. She had no idea why she was so surprised to hear Rahn converse in Arabic. After all, she'd just done it and she was a sistah from Colorado with no ties to this country to speak of. Rahn, on the other hand, had family here.

"Your aunt asked us to look out for you and your fiancée. She has been expecting you."

"Thank you, Lieutenant." A quick glance down at his watch was followed by a polite, "We must be going. We're due to meet my relative at the bazaar in less than half an hour. Thank you for escorting my, er, fiancée. It is much appreciated."

Chrys didn't say a word as he hustled her out of the building, across the courtyards and through the gates. No complaints here—the bazaar was exactly where she wanted to go anyway. She couldn't decide whether to grimace or roll her eyes when Mahpiya let a taste of Rahn's irritation slip through the bond they shared with both spirit guides. He was a very unhappy camper. Might have something to do with her exploring on her own. Oh well.

Linking her arm through his, she flashed a blinding smile and walked beside him to the carriage that would serve as their ride.

Rahn's anger crackled in the air. But damn it, she would never be a fragile flower. When would he see that? She hadn't intentionally upset him, but it was simply in her nature to do things on her own. Something Chrys was willing to work on, but certainly not changeable overnight. Besides, what was the harm in wandering around an old fort? The place crawled with guards anyway.

"Rahn, won't you speak to me?"

His answering growl spoke volumes. Damn, the man was otherworldly hot and hunky, even when he was pissed off.

"Baby, stop worrying. I was fine by myself. Besides, you've been attacked on this trip, not me."

Oops. The stiffening of his spine screamed "wrong thing to say". She tried to clean it up.

"Rahn, I'm not trying to diss you. It's just that I've been on my own forever. Taken care of myself forever. Even with Delaine for a mischievous cousin, we grew up in different states. I only got to enjoy getting into trouble with her once a year, on our annual trip to Grandma's on the reservation. I don't want you worried about me, and I promise to try harder to let you protect me. Just realize that my independence isn't meant to make you worry. It's just who I am."

Anguish was painted across his brow, but the expression in his clear brown eyes said he understood.

"And let's not forget I've got two big bad African lions in my head with their power at my call simply for the asking."

With a frustrated sigh and a rake through his stylishly cut hair, he said, "I guess I can't expect you to do all the adjusting in this relationship. I'll try to be a bit more understanding when your need to get into trouble surfaces. I can't promise I won't spank you afterward."

The man had the yummiest smile this side of creation. *Yep. Sin on legs*, she thought as his grin did her in.

With her arm still twined around his, she leaned in close and inhaled. Mmm, he always smelled so good. All male musk and spicy love. He must totally exude some kind of kinky pheromone, because she couldn't think of a time since they'd been reunited that she didn't want to jump his bones. With a husky sigh, she whispered in his ear.

"Besides, right here, right now is the last time we'll be alone for a while. Don't waste it being angry. We'll be at your aunt's house for three days? Three whole days of sleeping without you? Damn. I can't wait to get back to the ship so I can strip you and bathe every inch of your rock-hard body." Had he stopped breathing? Good. She grinned secretly and continued. "Then I'll straddle your perfect, manly, muscular thighs and slide down onto that delicious cock of yours."

Rahn met her gaze with a deadpan expression. Chrys wondered what he was thinking until a flash of pure lust zinged from his light brown eyes. That stare became potent enough to singe her eyebrows. A quick peek downward revealed the ridge rising in his pants.

All on their own, Chrys' slender fingers found their way to his groin and encouraged that ridge to grow a bit harder. All the way to the bazaar.

At their destination, the driver pulled the *hantour* up to a post where several other horse-drawn carriages were parked. Rahn paid the man, climbed down and tried to discreetly adjust himself.

"Damned woman."

"What?" she asked innocently. "What'd I do?"

"I don't have anything to cover this up." He nodded discreetly toward the impressive bulge pushing against his zipper. "I'm almost tempted to go buy some traditional men's clothing to hide this damned thing."

"Well, I happen to like that damned thing."

"While I'm glad you enjoy my cock, I don't particularly want it on display. And I don't even want to think about trying to walk right now."

She laughed. Couldn't help it.

A few clouds rolled in from the west, but it was still warm and balmy as they moved along. Turning a corner, Chrys screeched to a halt, biting the inside of her lip to keep her mouth from falling open.

The fabulous and unique scents and sounds of the bazaar hit her square in the face. Row after row of stalls and tents stretched out before them. This was heaven. Had to be. She'd never seen so many different items available in an open-air market. This was like the flea market from God! And she could haggle with the best of 'em.

Music floated from various directions. Some fast, some slow, all with the telltale hypnotic sounds of drums and pear-shaped stringed *oud* present in most music from this region. And so many oils and fragrances, it boggled the mind.

Aside from colorful hieroglyphs and drawings on leaf papyrus, there were paintings of pharaohs and their queens, ankhs, camels and such on black, brown and even bronze dyed leather. Rugs in every color and pattern imaginable, brass lamps, spices and perfumes, mother-of-pearl, silver and resin jewelry boxes. Another peddled heavy blown-glass oil lamps in a slew of vibrant colors with accompanying sweet, spicy and floral scented oils. Her favorite was a hand-blended mix of jasmine and vanilla with a touch of sandalwood and lemon. The aroma was so delicious, it even caught Rahn's attention for a second.

The stall next door was packed with curio accessories, including lead crystal tea sets and water pipes. Chrys snatched up a royal blue *hookah* pipe along with a small brick of mango and orange sticky tobacco from an endless selection, determined to try it. Maybe she'd become a *shisha* connoisseur instead of a flavored cigar lover.

So wrapped up in shopping and purposely ignoring the shuffling drag of poor Rahn's feet, Chrys almost missed her own stomach grumbling.

"Sounds like you could use a little something to eat."

"Gee, you think? Snarky doesn't become you, Rahn," she muttered with a smile as she pulled him to the next tent.

"Oh yeah? Since when?"

Good question.

But when they ran across several booths with intricately designed, embroidered head covers called *galabia*, Chrys just had to look around some more. The women manning the booth explained that the head cover was usually black or white when outside the home, but could be myriad colors when worn at home. She bought four of them.

"Woman, where in the world will you wear those when we get home?"

Wicked incarnate, she turned to her mate. "For your information, I can wear them all the time with…nothing else."

Rahn instantly relieved her of her mountain of purchases before his iron grip wrapped around her biceps. Rahn eased her around and through the milling crowd to a less populated section and into an empty booth. He released her long enough to tie the flaps closed and crowd her into the back room, again tying the flaps. God, he hoped this booth was empty for the day and not just empty for, say, the next five minutes.

"Rahn, what are you doing?" Chrys whispered, the corner of her mouth tipped up into a barely there grin.

"Minx. How 'bout showing me what you look like in

that scarf right now…and nothing else."

"What? No way. What if somebody comes?"

"Should have thought of that before you decided to tease me," he grinned with slow and deliberate intent.

"Oh please, give me a break," she snorted, growing hotter by the second. Brown eyes practically aglow with sizzling heat, the man moved with purpose and grace, stalking her all the way across the tent. The back of her knees began to sweat. *Oh god, please send a strong breeze to cool me down*, she prayed. Because in a few more seconds, her little white linen pants outfit would be soaked through with more than just her own sweat.

Stiff with concern of getting busted having sex in an Arabic country in someone else's tent, Chrys bit her lip to keep from moaning. Didn't help at all.

"Aaaah." The groan slipped out as she was turned around and bent over the nearest object. Rahn's warm, wet tongue left a cooling trail across the skin on the back of her neck as his strong hands reached around her body. God, she loved when he did that.

Her breasts were at instant attention. Hell, even if he hadn't lifted her blouse to caress them, they swelled so quickly she could almost feel the blood pumping through the veins underneath her skin.

The heat of the day couldn't hold a candle to the temperature spike caused by the hard flesh pressed against her ass. Correction, the bare crack of her ass.

When the hell had the man taken her pants down? But she was so wet so fast, when he pressed into her yielding flesh and filled her in one stroke, Chrys didn't give a damn about the methods he used to undress her.

The man was a machine, all hard, unyielding and perfectly tuned. And so totally able to hit the sweet spot deep inside her creaming pussy.

"Damn," she panted. "God, that's so good."

"This is all I think about if you're within a hundred meters of me. Sliding into your hot pussy. Diving into this cunt as deep as I can go. Then holding you close after."

"Oh god," she wailed. He was fucking her like she was his last piece of ass before he died. He took her hard and fast. And her orgasm spiraled up out of her belly just the same way—hard and fast.

And she loved every minute of it.

Nothing like an afternoon quickie in a public place to invigorate a sistah. Hell, it was even better than shopping.

* * * * *

Later, Rahn breathed an audible sigh of relief when he spotted his aunt moving through the crowd. She waved and smiled as she made her way over to them.

Slightly taller than Chrys, her hair was covered with a beautifully embroidered *galabia*. Smooth skin, barely a shade lighter than Chrys' cinnamon tones, was visible on her face and hands. So this was a relative, eh? She knew it was probably a girl thing, but found herself wondering if the rest of Rahn's relatives had such beautiful skin. With his half-British, half-Egyptian heritage, Rahn sported more of the too-much-cream-in-the-coffee tanned tones, and boy, did he wear it well. Chrys was sure she'd never met such a handsome, gorgeously built, muscle-toting, kissable man as hers. Okay, time to quit staring and drooling at Rahn and greet his aunt like she had some sense.

"It is so nice to meet you, Chrysalyn."

"Chrys, please."

"Thank you. Chrys it is. I am Sumanjah el Hattal. You may call me Aunt or simply Suman will do."

The barely noticeable crinkles around her eyes and mouth brought to mind a mix of mature wisdom and a zest for life. She kind of reminded Chrys of her own aunts back home, who still lived on the reservation in South Dakota. Women who looked after their family, passed on wisdom and stood firm in the face of adversity, smiling all the while. And even though those women were friendly and sweet, they didn't miss a thing and wouldn't hesitate to tell you about yourself. And you'd better not call them by their first name, either.

Aunt Suman turned to Rahn. "I cannot stay long, but I do have news for you. Unfortunately, none of it is heartening."

Rahn looked back and forth between the two women.

"Maybe it can wait until later? We still plan to stay with you and Uncle a few days."

"Yes, but…"

The man was clearly torn between wanting to get the news on a possible suspect, but not wanting to leave her side to do it. Chrys tried not to roll her eyes, honest she did. But off they went, rolling upward in frustration before she could stop them.

"Rahn, why don't you find me a cup of that delicious thick-as-axle-grease stuff you guys call tea. Or better yet, I'll get it. We passed a stand with some goodies just down that way."

"Chrys, no…"

"I'll get some tea. You talk to Aunt Suman and do your job. I'm not officially on this case and I know you can't discuss details while I'm present. It is kind of cool that your aunt is your informant." Then she turned with an outstretched hand and said, "Ms. Sumanjah, I look forward to spending time with you and your family."

"Chrys," Rahn warned, the words pushed through gritted teeth.

Oh, please. She chuckled. He scowled and she reminded him that it was unlikely that she was a target.

Rahn practically bellowed, "And you know that how, exactly?"

Chrys' blood ran cold, simply because she couldn't answer the question. Yet she was determined that he not worry so much about her. Besides, in all her years of service, she'd never fallen prey to a criminal or became a target. This case was no different. If anything, Rahn was more likely to be in danger, considering he was actually "working". She was just along for the ride.

"Rahn, on the way here you promised to try to give me a little breathin' room, remember? Look, what could possibly happen to me here? The place is stuffed with people hawking and buying wares. And I promise to stay within screaming distance, okay?"

He looked ready to take his promise back, but he snapped his mouth shut. Judging from his clenched teeth and matching fists, Chrys knew it had probably taken all his mental and physical strength to pin his lips together. Good, 'cause she'd said all she had to say about it.

Giving him her back, she went off in search of something to drink. The tea served here was so strong that even though it was meted out in a cup barely bigger than a shot glass, it required at least three teaspoons of sugar just to get it down. But it was delicious and would stave off her hunger a bit longer. Not to mention the wonders of caffeine.

Standing outside one of the small cafes with a permanent location at the bazaar, she sipped the steaming brew and winced. Damn, it was potent stuff. Mahpiya and Adonei had been on high alert ever since she left Rahn's side and it was beginning to get on her nerves.

Can't you two settle down? Or at least close down the link a little bit. Your edginess is making me nervous.

But Chrys' words only seemed to agitate them more. The next instant, both imposing spirits settled into a lion's most common battle stance—feet planted firmly, eyes pinned on what they perceived as a threat, and ready to pounce.

CHAPTER FIFTEEN

"Avoiding me?"

Chrys almost dropped her tea when the cats pacing around in her head upped their roaring and growling.

'Don't worry, you two. I'll be careful around him. He acts like a nice guy, but I'm beginning to have my doubts.'

For the first time in weeks, Chrys admitted to herself and her guides that there was something just a bit off about Eden, no matter how suave he appeared. Six years of undercover training kicked in and Chrys painted on a plastic smile and a serene façade. If she played her cards right, maybe she could get some answers in regard to what rubbed her companions the wrong way.

"Hi, Eden. Where've you been hiding lately? We didn't get a chance to thank you for helping after Rahn was injured."

"I thought I should give you and your friend some privacy to heal. I'm sure it was traumatic for you."

For her? Rahn was the one who'd been attacked. He was the one someone had tried to carve up like a Sunday baked turkey. Her man had lain in a pool of blood that night. If anything, it was traumatic for Rahn. She looked at Eden sideways, not caring for the irritation, however slight or unintended, when Eden called Rahn her friend.

Then there was Adonei. Damned lion was pacing the well-worn trail across her mind again.

Eden ordered a tea and asked, "So where is Mr. Benson?"

"Who? Oh, Rahn?" she asked with her best oblivious-as-a-blonde expression. "He's off shopping for a surprise for me," she lied. "Hey, what was that?"

"What was what, Chrysalyn?"

"That noise. Sounds like someone is in distress."

Instinct had her legs moving toward the sound. With a confused-looking Eden tagging behind her, Chrys silently sent Adonei ahead to scout.

When the mighty lion returned, his news hit her straight in the gut.

It's a female. She is under attack. Two males, both masked. Neither as strong as you, even without the infusion of my powers.

Chrys turned a corner into a dim alley and took in the scene before her. Just as Adonei said, two men yanked at the clothes of a kicking, screaming woman. She was completely covered from head to toe, like a Bedouin woman, but the creeps harassing her were trying to make sure she didn't stay that way.

Well, watching someone get raped in an alley just didn't float her boat. Without a second thought, Chrys moved in to protect the female and walked confidently into the fray. The men looked up and she could see their leers through the scarves over their ugly faces. One of them licked his lips. Ewww. Nasty bastard.

Eden's hastily mumbled "I'll go get help" made it more than clear she was on her own. Fine. Coward.

All their attention on Chrys, they released the woman who promptly took off at a dead run. The two would-be rapists began to circle Chrys. No worries. With no weapons, her body would simply have to take these assholes down.

Surrounded, Chrys didn't doubt she could still beat the hell out of them, especially with Adonei's strength. All she had to do was call.

Or that was the plan until Mahpiya shouted a warning into her skull. Too late. Someone snuck up behind Chrys and poked her in the kidneys with a very heavy, very cold piece of steel. Hell, even with lion super-strength and speed, there was no way she could dodge a bullet this close.

The order to shut up or else was an unfamiliar muffled hiss against her ear. And these bastards looked more than capable of following up on the "or else" part.

"Turn around."

Hands up in surrender, Chrys obeyed and mentally kicked herself in the head for not being more careful.

"What the hell?" she demanded, unable to keep the incredulity out of her voice. Eyes narrowed in disbelief, she stared at her abductor—Eden and the woman she'd just rescued. Even after swearing to be careful she'd allowed herself to be duped.

One of the bad guys wrapped several thin, but strong, twine ropes around her wrists and tossed a simple dress-like garment over her, effectively hiding her from the world. The victim had been nothing but bait and Chrys was well and truly caught. For now.

In the meantime, a call for Rahn was in order.

'Adonei, come to me. I need your assistance.'

I am here, my charge.

'Please go find Rahn. Show him what's happened. I need help.'

I am sorry, Chrysalyn, but I cannot.

'What?' she almost yelled aloud. 'What the hell do you mean? You can't scout him out and bring him back to help me?'

We both promised your mate we would not leave your side for any reason.

'You're my spirit guide, not Rahn's. Since when do his

wishes carry more weight than mine?' she snarled along the bond as Eden's goon squad hustled her through the empty alleyway and away from the bazaar.

Since you mated him, Adonei responded frankly.

'What? Oh, this is fucking ridiculous. Mah, can you go?'

The lioness refused. But it made more sense for her to refuse a request than Adonei.

I cannot disobey my charge any more than I can interfere in his choices. I was asked to stay with you and gave my word. But I promise to lend you my hunter's strength the moment your body is far enough away from the weapon trained on you.

You cannot lend her strength. Only I can do that, Adonei huffed indignantly.

Yet you will not do as your charge asks and go to her mate? Could you possibly get any more hypocritical than you are at this moment?

An argument ensued. Chrys couldn't believe it. She was being taken who-knew-where thousands of miles from home while her two supposed bad-assed lions fought over who should do what. Obviously, mating among humans with mated spirit guides was rare, but right now, Chrys couldn't care less about their hierarchical rules and laws.

'Somebody do something, damn it,' Chrys demanded. That stopped the argument but didn't get her any further. So it was time to talk some sense into these boneheaded cats once and for all.

Patience all but done, she argued the case that because they were joined, Mahpiya was as much her spirit guide as Adonei, and vice versa for Rahn. By the time the three of them got a decent plan formed between them, the sun was setting and they were well outside of the city.

From the front seat of the vehicle, the woman who'd lured her into the alley turned, pulled off her head cover and leaned over the seat. It was then Chrys realized that none of her captors, save Eden, were Egyptian. They were all Eastern European with classic Euro features. Made perfect sense.

Rahn had explained to her how men of his culture believed they were caretakers of the earth and their faith, which included women. No man worth his salt in this country would sit by and watch if she were in trouble. So, Eden had gotten someone else to do his dirty work.

Eden's arms came around her to hold her still as the woman stuck a needle into the fat vein at the side of her neck. Shit, it hurt. And she'd better not get an infection or she'd have to kick their asses twice, damn it. A slow burn spread from the injection site, erupted straight into her brain and sent her into oblivion.

* * * * *

Damn it, they'd looked everywhere. Mahpiya had been feeding Chrys' anger, and then her fear, through their bond. He at least knew the woman was all right. Then suddenly, it winked out. It was as if Chrys had disappeared off the face of the earth. He started to summon Mahpiya, but didn't want to call her away from his mate's side. Surely she was better off with two spirit guides rather than one.

All of his local family had gathered at Aunt Suman's home in anticipation of Rahn's homecoming, only to be met with the news that his fiancée was missing.

His aunt walked out onto the porch and put an arm around him.

"We will find her, Rahn. I promise."

She meant well and Rahn appreciated it. But it did nothing to quell the deep guilt he felt at allowing the damned woman to go romping around the bazaar alone. It didn't matter that she now had two spirit guides to keep her safe. He was ultimately responsible for her safety and happiness. Period.

"Thanks, Aunt Suman, I appreciate that." He knew his words were hard and angry, but he simply couldn't help it. Damn it, he was angry. Angry at himself for letting her out of his sight. Angry that someone had managed to tail her here, someone he should have caught by now. Angry for not realizing Chyrs was even in danger. She didn't fit the profile of the others who'd had their lives terminated at every port that damned ship stopped at. Why Chrys? Why her?

"I think I'll go for a walk, get into my own space so I can think a bit."

His aunt smiled in understanding and said, "All the family is here for you. And we are expecting a bit of help from an unexpected source."

"What unexpected source? Who?"

Rahn's eyebrows quirked in question, but she waved him off with a simple, "I'll tell you when you return from your walk if they have not arrived by then."

Rahn looked up at the sky as he went. It was so beautiful here. The sky was so clear, he didn't doubt he could see all the lights of the entire universe. But nothing compared to the sweet light in his woman's eyes. The way she brightened when he walked into a room. The way she reached for him, accepted him, both in and out of bed. And he realized Chrys would never allow him to lock her away from life, away from the world. She was a free spirit. But could they find a way for her to be both free and safe?

He kept walking, thinking of the sunset he'd watched alone and how Chrys would have enjoyed seeing the clouds morph from vivid reddish-orange to pinkish-purple to deep gray.

Down the block and around the corner, Rahn sucked in a deep, startled breath as Mahpiya's imposing presence literally roared into his head.

'Mah? What the hell are you doing here? You're supposed to be with Chrys.'

Adonei is watching over her. Since I am as much her spirit guide as I am yours, I must grant her request under these circumstances.

'What circumstances, Mah? What are you talking about?'

Mahpiya told him the whole sordid tale from beginning

to end, starting from the supposed bumping into Eden at the tea stand, to the woman Chrys had gone to help, to her present location and direction.

From hopeless concern to jubilation, he could barely contain himself. Because of Mahpiya, he now had everything he needed to rescue his woman. He was so damned grateful he couldn't even be angry at Mahpiya for leaving Chrys' side. Besides, Rahn was no fool. If Mah was here, she had good reason to be. The lioness was not just a great hunter, she was one of the wisest entities that walked the earth.

'Mah, show me what's happening now.'

As you wish, my charge.

Immediately, Mah's image faded from his mind and was replaced with the scene of a slumbering Chrys slouched in the backseat of a car.

Mahpiya's quiet voice caught and pulled him out of the vision she'd sent to him.

You are growling aloud, Rahn. Do not bring unnecessary attention to yourself.

And she was right. It wasn't as if he was the only one out on the streets of Alexandria tonight. He couldn't help Chrys if he was locked up in the loony bin for walking down the street talking to himself while *not* drunk.

Focusing again on the images flowing into his brain, Rahn understood one thing immediately. Chrys was asleep, but not because she wanted to be.

'What did they give her, Mah?'

These are some of the thoughts Chrysalyn sent me before she passed out.

Injectable sedative. Great. At least she would sleep through most of her ordeal.

'Show me the signs on the road.'

They were headed south on the main road toward Cairo. Considering the amount of time Chrys had been missing, Rahn was sure they'd almost completely covered the scant one hundred or so miles. If they hadn't already, they would soon.

Rahn's heart went out to his woman as Mah explained Eden's part in this play. And he'd bet his life that the bastard's role was bigger than they realized. But appearing to be helpful when Rahn was injured put Eden in Chrys' good graces, even against her better judgment. Now she was paying for it. And according to Mahpiya, his little hellion wasn't the least bit happy about it.

But he was still going to paddle her ass for walking into danger instead of calling for help. He'd do it with some understanding, of course, then follow up with hot sweaty make-up sex.

Your mate is more distraught for you than she is for herself. Then Mah opened the gate of her memories and let them flow through the bond shared with her new charge.

Chrys' thoughts and feelings poured into him. They completed and filled every nook and cranny of his soul. Rahn shook his head in awe, moved by the depth of love and anger his woman carried on his behalf.

'Mah, thank you for sharing my mate's feelings with me. But we have another problem.'

What is that, my charge? You will go to her infused with strength and purpose, a gift from your spirit guide. Adonei will do the same for your mate. I see no problem here.

'Except the one Chrys might create. I felt the heat behind the images you showed me. I know she's pissed off. And she's not afraid of a damned thing, even when she should be. I just know she'll say something stupid to those idiots holding her.'

There, you have a point. Adonei and I will see what we can do to keep things under control until your arrival. The cat sighed. *I must say, you are much less of a handful than Chrysalyn. And you are a male.* This was said with disbelief and a wink.

Rahn snorted.

The lioness was gone.

Rahn ate up the distance back to the house at a dead run. Simmering with anxiety, he tried to keep his anger from rising to a full boil. He would have his woman back and Eden would go down for the count. At any cost.

Toeing off his shoes, he rushed over the threshold and headed to the living area, where he knew his Aunt Suman, her sisters and all their husbands, along with a horde of cousins waited.

"Aunt Su…" His words trailed off.

Talk about shock. The room was not only full of his family. Off to one side stood six dark-haired men he didn't know personally, but could see a resemblance that spoke volumes over the sudden silence.

Eden's relatives. His brothers, to be exact. Last he heard, the apple didn't fall far from the tree. So if Eden was a pathological liar and psychopath, what were his brothers?

"Aunt Suman?" Rahn asked in a near snarl, nowhere near ready to trust these strangers, not with his woman's life.

"They have been, shall we say, assisting me in gathering intelligence for you. On their own brother."

"What?!"

She grabbed him by the ear—he'd hated that since he was a little boy—gently eased his face down to hers and whispered for his ears only. "They do not know who you work for or the details of your case, but when I ran the information past them on the possible suspect, all of them agreed that their brother, Eden Pall, fit the profile."

As Rahn listened carefully to his aunt's words, his gaze remained plastered on the man he perceived was the oldest. When she finished, she took a step back and waited.

"Why are you doing this?" Rahn asked, not bothering to keep the edge or skepticism out of his voice. He had no reason to trust these men. Not with his mate's life.

The eldest, a man named Adel, replied. "Because we are bound to protect life, just as your family is."

With a neutral expression, he silently wondered if the

man knew that he, his family and his woman were all agents of one kind or another?

"Even if it means reining in one of our own. We understand your woman is missing. Our youngest, Nasir," who waved his hand so Rahn would know who they were speaking about, "saw Eden at the bazaar today about the time your aunt says your woman disappeared. I know what it is like to lose a mate to unfortunate circumstances. We cannot support the actions of our sibling. We wish to assist."

The remaining men didn't say a word, just nodded their agreement.

Rahn accepted their help. They were here because of his aunt. The woman was no fool. She would have checked them out six ways from Sunday. Even down to their underwear size if need be. And because he trusted his aunt, he would extend the hand of friendship to these men. Until they blinked wrong.

He flipped open his emergency satellite phone and hit the speed dial.

"Geri, Chrys has been taken. I have a feeling her captor might be responsible for more than just making off with her. I've just received intel on where she is." He left out the part about being told this by his spirit guide. "Boss, I need a few favors."

With Mahpiya's road map imprinted firmly in his mind, a seething, determined Rahn and a small horde of equally determined males headed for Alexandria's El Nohza airport.

* * * * *

Awake, groggy and somewhat stiff, Chrys resisted the urge to stretch. The needlelike sensation shooting down her numb left butt cheek was a pretty good indication of just how long she'd been asleep.

It was comforting to have Mahpiya back in a quiet corner of her mind and Adonei standing watch ready to wake her if needed. As they slowed to a stop, she cracked her lids open just enough to realize it was pitch black outside. She almost grinned evilly at the big wet spot that spread from just underneath her chin to soak into the fabric of the man next to her. She might not be able to fight Eden, his goons and the goonette right now, but she'd sure slobbered on him good.

Mahpiya's chuckle sounded behind her ear and Chrys bit her lip to keep from answering in kind. It was childishly funny, but hell, she'd take what she could get right now.

The car slowed to a stop, then took off again. Chrys sat up with a jolt.

What the hell? Or rather where the hell?

Unlike the more traditional old-styled neighborhoods of Alexandria, this place was a bustling, brightly lit, tourist-filled metropolis. Street vendors pushed their carts along. Couples strolled the boulevard holding hands, some shopping, others having coffee or tea in one of the many outdoor shops. Wow, a soaring statue of Ramses III sat atop a pedestal that seemed to rise up out of nowhere and was lit from underneath by small spotlights. The walls of shops and apartments were covered with colorful paintings and mosaics.

The foliage-lined, wide sidewalks were full of life, both old and young. But the streets? Holy shit, it was worse than driving in New York!

Chrys almost wished she'd stayed asleep. There wasn't a stoplight to be seen, and even when someone was crossing the six lanes of traffic, none of the drivers slowed. Only honked loudly and continued right on through what should have been crosswalks.

Just when she thought they'd splatter someone all over the pavement, they turned off the main road, left the more populated streets and headed into a quieter neighborhood.

Hmm. No hustle or bustle here. Instead, all was eerily quiet, almost tomblike.

Their car pulled over and parked near a low arch cut into a high wall. Eden and the skanky female hopped out of the car. Left in the backseat alone, panic pushed at the edges of Chrys' mind when the two goons approached the still-open rear door. Adonei sent soft reassurance through the bond.

Rest easy, Chrysalyn. Your mate will arrive shortly.

The typical quiet calm that encompassed her in times of danger was under siege by an almost unreasonable fear. Fear of never seeing Rahn again. Fear of never resting her back against his chest as he held her, surrounding her with his strength and warmth.

And that pissed her off.

Chrys twisted and pulled against the still-tight bonds. Searing pain sizzled through the nerve endings of her wrists and hands, clear down to the fingertips. Damn, that hurt.

'How long before Rahn gets here?'

An hour perhaps.

'Good,' Chrys growled along the link. 'Then I have an hour to get free and kick some Eden ass.'

Mahpiya padded forward in Chrys' head and sat down beside Adonei. *Your mate does not doubt your ability to win against your captor, but he would rather you do something more important.*

'Like?' she snapped.

Like getting this Eden person to talk.

Understanding lit through her. Determination to assist her mate and take Eden down pushed every other thought from her mind. Chrys gritted her teeth and forced herself not to pull away from the man reaching into the car. He hauled her out of the vehicle, down the street and through the arch into bleak nothingness.

CHAPTER SIXTEEN

'Adonei, please assist me.'

The tawny head of the regal lion nodded in acknowledgement of her request. Agitated and beyond ready for action, Adonei growled, *Take what I offer, my charge.*

A burst of raw power pumped into Chrys' body, blitzed through her blood and burst through each muscle fiber. Her senses flared alive. The outline of the tombs and dimly lit narrow pathways, when met with the infusion of the lion's enhanced sight, appeared sharper, more defined. Crystal clear was the stern jawline of thug number one as he jerked her along and the wide back of thug number two walking ahead of them. The putrid stench of rotting garbage and raw sewage forced her gag reflex to tighten her throat. Taking shallow breaths, Chrys parted her lips to breathe through her mouth. Bad move. She could practically taste the muck on her tongue.

Overflowing with the strength of the mightiest hunters, Chrys snapped the bindings around her wrist with a simple flick, careful to keep her hands in a bound position. The garment they'd tossed over her earlier while hustling her out of the bazaar hid her freedom.

Vermin scurried out from underfoot as their party ducked through an entrance and into a small dwelling. The escorting bad guy gave her a shove. Pretending to stumble, she fell into a chair in the center of a shadow-shrouded room. A light clicked on and Chrys froze.

They were in a fucking tomb. Literally.

"Eden, where the hell are we?" Chrys demanded.

The thugs and thugette disappeared through an exit across the room, leaving her and Eden alone.

Sitting stiffly, back ramrod straight, Chrys demanded answers as Eden circled her like a buzzard waiting for the fresh meat to drop. Moments ticked by and she wondered if he would answer at all. Finally, the man spoke in a quiet, emotionless flat tone. So flat it brought to mind a vivid image of some poor soulless automated robot, unfeeling, uncaring as it floated in the blackness of space toward nothingness.

A single finger trailed over her shoulders and across the back of her neck as he moved around and around her still body.

"We are in Qarafa." At her blank stare, he continued. "What Westerners would call The City of the Dead."

"The who?"

"The City of the Dead," he repeated in a disconcerting flat-sounding timbre. "This place was an important burial ground hundreds of years ago, now the poor gather here. Thousands of them. Just think, among soaring minarets, mosques, elaborate tombs of sultans and their families, live ordinary men and women. In fact, a lovely widow lives in a tomb room just a few doors down with her children."

"But, but how?" Chrys stammered. Not from nervousness—she was too angry for that—but from the simple inability to fathom anyone living in a place like this.

"We have not so much thought of cemeteries as a place of the dead, but rather a place where life begins," Eden replied. "The new tenants have adapted where the families of the dead used to come to spend time with their departed loved ones. Now the grave markers serve as desks and shelves, while strings hung between gravestones are used to dry laundry. As for the light, they've brought in the electricity by wires over the roofs coming from the nearby mosque. Pity, really."

Well, the name certainly fit the place. The City of the Dead—northern Cairo's four-mile-long walled necropolis that now housed thousands of families and countless small businesses. In this day and age? Amazing.

But it didn't explain why the hell he'd brought her here. Not to mention he seemed too refined to have a "room" in this place for any virtuous purpose.

"But why…?"

"She thought I was wrong, you know. But I wasn't, it was her. She'd made the mistake, stupid bitch."

Okay, the words insane and crackpot came to mind. Chrys bit her tongue and let the man rant.

"Even pharaohs make mistakes. Sometimes deadly ones. But it really doesn't matter. With you at my side, I have no need of another pharaoh or harem mistress. The tarot was connected to the Rahn asshole after all."

Then Eden threw back his head and laughed as if the funniest joke in all of creation had just been told. Oookay? When the cackling ceased, Chrys took a slow breath, forced her words to emerge meek and humble.

"What tarot, Eden? I'd really like to understand."

Hmm. That seemed to please the walking nut job.

With a smile, he stopped circling and stopped in front of her. From his left breast pocket, he removed a beautiful card covered with gold, black and lapis blue Egyptian symbols and hieroglyphs.

"It was the Empress. This card represents the Empress, see? I always selected different, and sometimes unusual, suits of cards, but she always explained them to me. But after I saw you for the first time aboard ship, I kept selecting this same card over and over. And always upside down. Stupid pharaoh had me believing it was because you were losing interest in the Rahn asshole."

The bottom of Chrys' stomach danced with unease. Now this was getting freaky. Right, as if Eden weren't already in that category. She held her thoughts to herself, demanded her fists to remain still. Giving away the fact that her hands were no longer tied would probably make the man stop talking.

And that simply wouldn't do. Her mate wanted a confession and, damn it, she was going to get him one.

"But you weren't losing interest in him," Eden rounded on her with a snarl. "You had no interest in me. But that will change, I promise you. I still don't understand why he didn't die." Eden's head tilted just a hair to the right, his expression one of genuine bewilderment.

"Die?" Chrys uttered in shock, and this time was no act.

"Yes, die, damn it all. He was supposed to die. I know I cut him in the right spot. But you came and did something to him. What did you do to him? All I wanted to do was stomp his brains out when I came into your apartment and saw you covered with his blood. You were moving toward the phone to call for help while that damned Rahn moaned like a foaling cow on the bathroom floor."

Chrys fought for calm, begging her spirit guides to send her a large dose and fast. Adonei's power still pulsed through her body and she fought to keep her temper under control, fought to keep the fierce force of the lion leashed.

But the more he talked, the more she wanted to rip his head off.

Keep calm, Chrysalyn. He baits you, Mahpiya crooned. *This must be finished before your mate arrives.* Then she flashed a quick glimpse of Rahn and a whole host of mean-looking men with him. And they were close.

Eden was pacing again, his words distant and far away, as if he were trying to work something out in his head. "I just don't understand. I cut all the other specimens in the exact same spot, and they all died within minutes. Perhaps it was because Rahn is more muscular, larger than the females I gutted? Or maybe I missed the spot all together."

"What specimens, Eden?"

"The women. I know you know about the women, Chrysalyn. My pharaoh hand-picked them all, one in each port of call. All strong, independent, capable. None of them needed to be led, but none were willing to follow. Too eager to step on the back of a male. Not like you, Chrysalyn. You are strong, yet understand the need to walk beside a man as an equal. Not afraid to be a real woman loved by a man. There is no desire to trample on him. On me."

Boy, did he have that last part wrong! She'd trample him, all right. Son of a bitch. The bastard was behind it all—the attacks at each port, the attack on Rahn and now, her abduction. By appearing to be helpful, he'd diverted suspicion away from himself. And since the spirit guides had never liked him, Chrys had simply gotten used to them going ballistic whenever the man was in the room.

And Eden had almost succeeded in adding Rahn to his list of victims. While her man had lain prone on that bathroom floor, bleeding to death. Spiritual law dictated that spirit guides be called or summoned onto this plane. Their assistance had to be requested. Something Rahn couldn't have done while unconscious.

Bad guy or not, without Eden's help that night, Rahn could very well be hanging around in the spirit realm with Mahpiya and Adonei.

And this idiot, perplexed and angry because Rahn hadn't kicked it that night, now confessed everything. She had all they needed to bring this asylum candidate to justice.

Just then, Eden moved in close enough for her to hear the air move in and out of his lungs. Then the man began moving down a different, more bizarre path. With a gentle touch, a single finger lovingly traced a path along Chrys' jawbone.

"Chrysalyn, I am pleased with you. You will be my queen forever, and bear me strong sons."

His eyes were alight with love and determination. Shit, the man was serious. How could someone so handsome, articulate and educated turn out to be such a nut job?

A slithering crawl eased along her skin when Eden's hand came in contact with her shroud-covered breast.

Waiting for Rahn dropped off the list of options.

* * * * *

Adonei broadcast everything going on in that damned room right into Rahn's head as he and his backup waited outside the tomb room door. The second he saw that Eden bastard put his hands on Chrys, it was all he could do not to rush in and just start shooting. Except gunfire was a last resort for all of them. It was illegal to live in this place, but it was packed with people. Every empty tomb sheltered a person or a family, all very much alive. They couldn't risk having shots sound here. The Egyptian government might turn a bit of a blind eye to the people squatting here, but gunfire was something they would definitely investigate. And fast.

There are three armed humans in the back room, Adonei warned.

'Any other way in?'

There is no other entrance to this dwelling.

'Well, we can't go in with guns blazing. Not with Chrys in the line of fire between us and them. Tell her to duck 'n cover. Right fucking now.'

The lion's presence winked out and Rahn called out to his guide. Mahpiya immediately responded, pouring supernatural strength and ability into his mind and body until it overflowed every nerve, every cell. Seconds later, he kicked in the door and rushed the room along with all six of Eden's brothers.

Eden snatched his hand away from Chrys' breast as if he'd been well and truly caught...which he was. The flash of recognition that lit his dark eyes was quickly replaced with a hard look, full of resentment and crazed determination.

Time slowed to a crawl. Chrys hit the floor and covered her head at the exact moment Rahn stormed in. Two big rugby-looking, rough-hewn European trees and a dark-haired woman flew in from the other side of the room and threw themselves into the fray.

Infused with the strength of the lion, an unarmed Rahn took evasive action and was across the room before the obviously inexperienced bad guy wannabe could get a shot off. But when he did fire, it echoed around the tomb with a deafening boom. Eden's brothers took down the other two and headed for Eden.

But not before he'd practically climbed on Chrys' back while she was still in a crouch on the floor.

"Hold it right there. One more and she joins the others."

All eyes, except the ones of the unconscious rogues, focused on the glint of the wicked blade pressed just underneath Chrys' jaw.

"Hold on now, brother," Adel called softly. "It's us. We are all here."

Eden's wild-eyed glare raked over his brothers.

"Why are you here, Adel?"

"We have come to help you."

"Really? It seems more as if you were helping him." Eden motioned his head toward Rahn, who managed to take a couple of steps his way while he'd been focused on his siblings. Just another step or two and Rahn could take him. Had to.

As if he'd read Rahn's thoughts, he pulled Chrys tighter against his body and pressed the blade closer. Close enough to cause an almost imperceptible thin line of blood, almost as fine as a cat's scratch, to appear.

Oh god, what could he do? What should he do? One wrong move and his woman would die before his eyes.

Before he'd had a chance to say and do all the things he'd missed out on for the years they'd been parted.

No, this was simply unacceptable.

His fists flexed and his heart drummed in his ears. He'd pounded one of the rogues into a pulp in no time flat. He'd just have to find a way to do the same to Eden. With Mahpiya's strength, he just might make it.

Shit. The odds simply weren't good enough.

'Mahpiya, I need your wisdom.'

Your mate has a plan.

'Share it with me.' In a flash, the details streaming through Chrys' mind moved from her to Adonei to Mahpiya to Rahn. Rahn felt the color drain from his face.

'No. Tell her no fucking way is she to try…'

Then Chrys moved, infused with Adonei's essence.

One hand grabbed Eden's wrist so fast and hard that the knife clattered to the stone floor. Before anyone could get within two strides of Chrys, she had the man knocked out, subdued facedown on the floor with her knee jammed into the back of his neck.

And she was shaking like a leaf.

He went to her then, gathered her up in his arms and held her tight. He felt the exact moment when shock and reality of what could have happened gripped her. With her face buried in his shirt, he spoke in hushed tones.

"Take deep, steady breaths, baby. It's all right. It's over now."

"Rahn, he tried to take you away. And he, he killed all those women…"

"I know, love. But you stopped him. Stopped him cold."

Her teeth were chattering now as the adrenaline crash let her down hard. Adonei and Mahpiya both retreated slowly, careful not to jar either of their charges.

God, he would never let her out of his sight again. Not even to take a pee. If he had his way, he'd just keep her chained to the bed with his head buried between her legs.

He'd make her come so hard she couldn't walk or talk, let alone leave by herself on a mission.

Shit, he'd never been so scared. Twice in his career he'd faced certain death, and he'd rather face it again than see Chrys in the hands of a criminal.

Adel bounced him out of his current train of thought.

"Quickly, go now. We will take care of cleaning up. You must clear the area before the police arrive. You cannot be found here."

Rahn reached out and clasped hands with each man, from the eldest to the youngest. "I understand. Thank you for your help tonight. We are in your debt. We couldn't have done this without you."

"I'm not sure about that, friend," Adel said with a grin. "You and your woman move like nothing I have ever seen. Perhaps when we meet again, you will teach me this, yes?"

With a smile and a slight bow, Rahn bundled up a shivering Chrys and disappeared into the darkness.

EPILOGUE

Now this was heaven.

No phones. No laptops. No work. Just Chrys moaning her pleasure around his cock as she flexed her jaw muscles while her mouth surrounded him.

Back arched into the moment, Rahn briefly—very briefly—thought on the events of the past three weeks.

After taking Eden down, Chrys had given all the details of the man's bizarre killing spree to Rahn's family and Eden's brothers. Before the Egyptian secret police arrived in the City of the Dead, Chrys had been spirited away— wouldn't do for an American agent to be caught "working" in Egypt without permission. Rahn and his Aunt Suman looked on with respect as Eden's brothers turned him over to the police. To tie up any loose ends, Eden's oldest brother walked into a holding cell and got the man to repeat, with chilling detail, every murder he'd committed. Some they hadn't even known about. And with diplomats present from several of the countries where the crimes were committed, including Portugal, Spain, France, Italy and Greece, Eden hadn't had a chance of fighting extradition. In the end, they'd all agreed he was beyond rehabilitation. Eden Pall was currently enjoying a full range of sedatives and anti-hallucinogenics in an undisclosed location.

And Rahn lay on a towel in the solarium on the top floor of his, now *their*, London flat. The sun warmed every inch of his gloriously naked body, with the exception of the parts the future Mrs. Chrys' torso cast shadows over. And those parts were warmed by her talented tongue and deep throat.

Damn, but the woman knew how to suck a cock. Went down on him like she'd never get enough. The perfect O of her lips encircled the tip the same way they did one of her favorite flavored cigars. And the woman knew her way around a good cigar.

Her tongue flicked over, teased and licked his lollypop before covering him completely. Over and over again, she sucked and laved until his balls practically crawled up his back.

"Damn, Chrys. God, that feels so good. Yeah, suck it, baby."

Her hums and moans became frantic, sending a wicked vibration through his cock and sac. Rahn loved the way she got all hot and bothered from giving him head. He knew if he reached down and stroked her pussy, she'd be soaked and ready for him.

A strong hand slid over the ridges of his abs and up to tweak a stiff male nipple. The other followed her talented mouth up and down his stiff length. The woman's whole body was into what she was doing, hips wriggling, back arched. She mumbled around him, her breath both cooling and warming his throbbing length.

"Mmm, you taste so good," she panted. "All male and musky and…mine."

Between wet swirls of her tongue and equally wet draws on his flesh, the words spilled out and sent his heat level soaring.

"I'm so hot right now." Suck. "My pussy is aching." Slurp. "Oh god, I need it."

How he loved it when she talked dirty. He loved it even more when she followed through. Chrys crawled up his body. The next instant, Rahn gasped with pleasure, balls-deep inside scalding-hot, wet, willing woman. And she rode him until the cream of her cunt frothed around the base of his rod.

"Oh yeah, Chrys. Give me that pussy, baby. Fuck me."

"Yes. Rahn. Mmmm…" Each word rose in volume and intensity until she yelled her pleasure. He shattered into a million pieces as her juicy sex rippled and gripped, pulling his own orgasm from the base of his cock.

Holding her tight to his chest, Rahn kissed the wild riot of curls on top of her head. The Great Spirit had truly blessed him.

He had two African lions, strong and regal, for spirit guides. A job he loved. And the most special woman on earth, his equal professionally, spiritually and definitely in the bedroom. And he loved her to the depths of his soul. More than he could have ever imagined loving another human being.

And he'd found her in the most unlikely of places.

On an Egyptian voyage.

ALSO BY AUTHOR TJ MICHAELS

Carinian's Seeker
Book One in the Vampire Council of Ethics series.
Serati's Flame
Book Two in the Vampire Council of Ethics series.
Hatsept Heat
Book Three in the Vampire Council of Ethics series.
Wild Winter Anthology
Feral Fascination Anthology
Gift Wrap Optional
Jaguar's Rule
Spirit of the Pryde

Turn the page for a preview of TJ Michael's award-nominated book paranormal romance that brings the wilds of the jungles of Belize up close...and very personal:

JAGUAR'S RULE
CHAPTER ONE

The big male swatted at the female's head but missed. She'd eluded his huge paw, jumped to the side of the unconscious human lying face down on the ground, his blood mingling with the wet grass. The female crouched again, ready to spring and prepared to fight for the human. He didn't doubt he could take her, but the set of her powerful shoulders and the gleam of the moonlight off her bared canines made him think twice. He'd seen this particular female before, often out in the jungle. None of the other males ever approached her. Perhaps she was a formidable foe?

But he wasn't just another male. He was a prime of his species, a jaguar, a fully grown *panthera onca* who always got what he wanted. He decided he wanted her.

She thought he was after the body she guarded. Good, let her. He would back off for now, taking the opportunity she'd unknowingly given him to watch her closely and see just what kind of female he was dealing with. But he had no doubt that in the end, she would find herself underneath him while he thrust with powerful strokes into her body. Oh yes, she would yield. He would see to it. And perhaps afterward, he would keep her.

* * * * *

Uhhnnn, owww. Aaron was sure someone had split his head open and used a metal baseball bat to work sand into the wound. And those voices! God, why wouldn't they just shut up? The buzz overlaying the words of whoever needed to shut up drilled through his brain.

Each breath sucked into his lungs felt shallow, as if he couldn't drag in enough air, and every breath out left behind a tight burning sensation. Why couldn't he take a deep breath and hold it? Pain this intense could only mean one thing—he was dying.

The voices were louder now. Damn it. Ready to glare at the people talking when his head pounded like a drum at a rock concert, he was somewhat surprised at the gritty feel behind his lids as he forced them open. He blinked then blinked again, but the blurry images wouldn't clear. They just moved back and forth in the dimly lit room. The sound of a million cawing birds filled his ears, and the sweet scent of wet grass floated on a cooling breeze across his skin. His *bare* skin. Did they have bare skin in the hereafter?

He blinked a few more times, wincing as the side of his head exploded with a new round of pain. And who was the bearded old man leaning close to his face? He wanted to lift his hand to smack the man and tell him to back up a bit. The garlic on his breath made Aaron's stomach lurch but the pounding in his head was so fierce, just the thought of blowing chunks made him grit his teeth to hold back the bile while the vein in his forehead threatened to burst. The old man was speaking. What? Sounded something like mud, or blood, or…he just couldn't make it out, his thoughts were too scrambled. Oblivion had been pretty sweet compared to this. Perhaps he could slip back into it?

But not before he caught a glimpse of the angel

standing just behind the garlicky old man. Now he remembered, sort of. Lightning. His plane had gone down in the jungle after the engine under the left wing caught fire. The image was blurry but he knew an angel when he saw one. Was she here to take him to heaven? He was sure he'd done at least a few good deeds to warrant making it through the pearly gates.

This angel had milk chocolate skin and a set of piercing, almond-shaped, light gray eyes that made his pulse skip a beat or two. And her hair, a shoulder-length mane any woman would kill for. Thick and curly, it hit her shoulders at the perfect length and made his fingers want to reach out and touch the silky black-as-sin tresses before he floated away to the hereafter. The image of his angel wavered.

"Wait! Come back, beautiful! Can't we spend some time? Maybe talk awhile before I leave this plane?" Could she hear his urgent whispers? Of course she could, all supernatural beings had great hearing. So why didn't she respond? Instead, she just looked at him with a strange mix of pity and irritation. What the hell kind of angel was she anyway? She was supposed to be smiling at him, preparing him for his journey. Well, she obviously wasn't interested in doing her job. Maybe if he lodged a formal complaint with God, she'd get fired.

The garlic master was back. His stomach lurched. *Damn it, old man*, he shouted in his head, and immediately regretted the ferocity of his thoughts. Now his neck, shoulders and ribs joined his head, pounding relentlessly against his skin from the inside out.

The older man stuck him on the top of his hand with something and the beauty faded away fast, but not before he got a good glimpse of the swell of the angel's breasts and the curve of her shoulders. Since when did cherubs wear tank tops? It sure looked good on her. And how could be he in so much pain and still manage to achieve a hard-on? *Damn, she's sexy*, he smirked at himself as his eyelids fluttered closed. Hell, even in his state of impending death, he was thinking with his cock instead of his brain.

I'm no better than the half-assed angel, he thought as sleep claimed him.

* * * * *

Reya followed Dr. Matons out of her bedroom and closed the door with a quiet snap. After brewing herself a cup of tea, she joined her old friend out on the screened veranda and plopped down in her favorite plastic patio chair. The smell of the passing storm was heavy in the air, along with the scent of charred wood and jet fuel. In spite of the evening's hair-raising events, she was calm and determined.

Vanilla and clove scented smoke floated up from Dr. Matons' pipe. She should have never asked her Aunt Sulu to send the stuff. Now the old curmudgeon would never again settle for the local tobaccos.

"Well, our little patient was lucky tonight," Dr. Matons drawled around his pipe.

"*Little* patient?" Reya queried with amusement. She was sure she'd never met a man so long his feet practically hung off the edge of her bed, or a more muscularly perfect specimen as the one lying in her bedroom. She and Dr. Matons had spent the past several hours removing glass and plastic from various patches of skin. They'd stitched the deeper cuts across his back, wrapped his chest tightly and cleaned off all the blood. She'd seen every inch of his magnificent body and there was nothing, and she meant *nothing*, little about him.

"It's a good thing you were out on patrol when his plane went down. I don't know if he would have made it otherwise," the doctor said, blowing out a ring of thick smoke. "He is certainly handsome, as men go." His eyes crinkled at the sides as he watched her. The old matchmaker. Always looking for someone to pair her up with. Even an unconscious man in serious condition.

When she didn't answer but stared out into the night, he continued. "I gave him a strong painkiller, but he's not out of the woods. Do you mind if I sleep here so I can check on him during the night?"

"No, I don't mind at all. Why don't you take the office? The futon in there is pretty comfy. I'll take the couch." Her eyes hadn't strayed from the tangle of ferns and vines leading into the dark canopy of jungle no more than a hundred yards from her back stairs.

"You're not planning on going back out in this deluge, are you?"

"The storm is almost past. I'll be fine. Besides, something weird happened out there tonight. If you're still awake when I get back, I'll tell you about it."

The moon, pale and obscured by dark thunderheads, was the only light shining onto her second-story veranda. Reya unlaced her boots, toed them off and set them beside the screen door that led down the back stairs. Dr. Matons continued to puff on his pipe while she peeled off her tank top and blood-spattered pants, tossed them in a pile and loosely tied a small bundle around her neck.

"Be careful, my dear. Wake me when you return," Dr. Matons called quietly. Extinguishing his pipe, he rose and slipped through the sliding glass door and into her living room.

Reya watched his retreating back until the subtle snap of the office door told her she was alone. Shirt, pants and shoes in a neat pile on the floor, she dropped to her knees. Muscles rippled and bunched as raw power surged through her limbs—heady, thunderous power as her body shortened then stretched. Her tall frame shuddered as thick fur burst through her pores, replacing smooth skin. The cooling breeze ruffled the sleek fur on the tufts of the ears of a black jaguar as she stalked down the stairs and loped into the surrounding jungle.

About the Author

TJ is an award-winning author of several romance genres, including paranormal, fantasy, sci-fi and urban fantasy romance. Writing like a madman, TJ hasn't lost steam. Her mind? Yep, that's gone, but steam there is a-plenty. A true Taurus, TJ isn't slowing down and she's definitely too stubborn to stop when she sees the fence!

No matter the genre TJ is penning, her favorite thing to do is build worlds. To take you somewhere extraordinary. To transport you to a place where you can close your eyes and slip into your fantasy...